W9-BLZ-302

THE
ORPHAN'S TENT

Books from Byron Preiss Visual Publications and
Atheneum Books for Young Readers:

LETTERS FROM ATLANTIS
by Robert Silverberg

THE DREAMING PLACE
by Charles de Lint

THE SLEEP OF STONE
by Louise Cooper

BLACK UNICORN
by Tanith Lee

CHILD OF AN ANCIENT CITY
by Tad Williams and Nina Kiriki Hoffman

DRAGON'S PLUNDER
by Brad Strickland

WISHING SEASON
by Esther M. Friesner

THE WIZARD'S APPRENTICE
by S. P. Somtow

GOLD UNICORN
by Tanith Lee

BORN OF ELVEN BLOOD
by Kevin J. Anderson and John Gregory Betancourt

THE MONSTER'S LEGACY
by Andre Norton

THE ORPHAN'S TENT
by Tom De Haven

THE ORPHAN'S TENT

TOM DE HAVEN

Illustrated by Christopher H. Bing

A Byron Preiss Book

Atheneum Books for Young Readers

THE ORPHAN'S TENT

Atheneum Books for Young Readers
An imprint of Simon & Schuster Children's Publishing Division
1230 Avenue of the Americas
New York, NY 10020

Copyright © 1996 by Byron Preiss Visual Publications, Inc.
Text copyright © 1996 by Tom De Haven
Illustrations copyright © 1996 by Christopher H. Bing

Cover painting by Christopher H. Bing. Cover design by Brad Foltz
Edited by John Betancourt

Special thanks to Jonathan Lanman, Howard Kaplan, and
Keith R. A. DeCandido.

All rights reserved, including the right of reproduction in whole
or in part in any form.

First edition
Printed in the United States of America
10 9 8 7 6 5 4 3 2 1

ISBN 0-689-31967-3

Library of Congress Card Catalog Number: 96-83225

1

"Kill me," said Ike Fuelle (pronounced *fuel,* like the stuff consumed to produce energy), "but I'm glad she didn't come back."

"Liar," Alice replied. Both of them, sister and brother, were blonds with ruddy cheeks and eyes so pale a blue-gray they seemed the color of smoke. She was wearing a cropped maroon T-shirt, khakis, and green canvas sneakers. Everything clean, crisp, very neat. Ike had on, as he'd had for the past three days, a pilly gray sweatshirt, baggy jeans, gym socks, and black workboots.

"Swear to God!" he said. "I'm glad Del's gone! Totally. And you should be glad, too."

"How can you even *say* that? She's our friend."

"She's a flake! And she's ungrateful. And this proves it, so that's that. I'll find somebody else who can sing. Don't think I won't."

"Blah-blah-blah."

"Because I *will*! And something else," said Ike. "Whatever Del left behind—her guitar, for instance?—we figure is rightfully ours. And we sell it."

"I'll sell *you*. Why do you got to talk like such a big twit? Know what I think? It's this guy, it's hearing about this guy Jude that she met. You're jealous, Ikey."

"That," he said, "is the dumbest thing I ever heard you say. And seeing as how you've said a whole *bunch* of dumb things in your stupid life, that," he said, "is something. And don't call me Ikey."

"Struck a nerve," she said, "struck a nerve!"

"Yeah, right. In your dreams."

At that point, Steve Fletcher (Fletch to everybody) stood

up and cleared his throat. He'd been sitting on a stool behind the cashier's counter, taking periodic swallows from his carton of coffee and listening, with a deadpan expression, to Ike and Alice bicker.

"Are you two loving sibs just about finished now?" he asked sourly. Fletch folded his arms across his chest. Bodybuilder arms, bodybuilder chest. He was wearing his "Allen's Garage" T-shirt, the one that read "Free Insurance Estimates" on the back. His knuckles were grouted with oil and grease. "You finished? Excellent! Then hows about we all just talk this thing over, all four of us, and get it done with?"

"Fine," said Ike.

Carefully, Alice gave a careless shrug. "Sure."

"Excellent! Hey, Bo? Wanna come join us?"

Bo Cudhy stood down at the far end of the store, flicking through T-shirts. He pulled a bright green one off the rack and held it up by its plastic hanger. With a smile, he studied the busy graphic screened on the front, then twirled it around to look at the band logo emblazoned on the back: Better Than Ezra.

"Bo?"

"Yeah, comin'," he said and reracked the shirt.

They were all gathered that morning—it was a Thursday in late September of 1995—in Alice Fuelle's narrow little record store, called We Got It.

The place was painted a royal purple, but you'd never have noticed unless you looked carefully, since every wall above the CD bins and the cassette racks, the seven-inch-vinyl dumps, and the listening table with its boom-box and headphones was papered over with riotously bright posters, stickers, and concert flyers. So were the front door and the plate windows.

Alice's shop, which specialized in alternative music, grossed between eight and eleven thousand dollars a month, barely enough to pay the rent, the bills, the taxes, and a modest salary to herself. At this stage in her life, though—

she was twenty-two, three years older than Ike—that's all she wanted.

Except in summer, there never was much business before three or three-thirty in the afternoon, when the local high schools let out. But that never stopped Alice—who'd always been the serious, "responsible" Fuelle; Ike, the opposite— from opening every morning at ten o'clock sharp.

Now it was five past eleven, and Fletch was talking. "The way I figure it," he said, "Del's a big girl. She can do whatever she likes. So I don't know from Ike's attitude. But—"

"Oh, you don't?" Ike said hastily. "I've got time and money invested in that girl!"

Fletch looked at him. The look said *shut up*, and it worked.

"But," Fletch continued, "I have to tell you guys, I'm starting to feel a little worried myself. I only wish she'd called."

"Exactly!" said Alice. "Why hasn't she? Something's wrong, that's why! She could be in real trouble."

"She could even be, like, dead," Bo said, then flinched. His big moon face turned bright crimson when Alice and Fletch, and even Ike, turned and glared at him. "It's possible!" he added defensively. Glancing down at his old gray Nikes, he discovered, and played at being fascinated by, a smear of dried toothpaste on the left toecap.

He rolled his eyes up slowly to see if they were still looking at him. They were—so he took off his Joe Camel gimme cap and whacked it against the side of his leg. That killed a few more seconds. At last, using both hands, he replaced the cap, backward naturally, and askew. "Sorry. Just forget I said anything. She's *fine*."

"I'm ninety-nine percent sure that she is," said Fletch. "But it *has* been ten days—"

"Eleven," said Alice.

"Eleven. Okay. So maybe we should—I don't know, call the cops?"

"In Richmond, Virginia?" Alice said.

"Why not?" said Bo. "They got phones."

"I got a better idea. We go down, and find her."

Ike threw up his hands. "It's an eight-hour drive!"

"I'll pay for the gas. Cheapskate."

"That's not the point, Alice! And you know it's not."

"I'll go," said Bo. "They talk funny down there. I like it."

"When were you thinking of leaving, Alice?" Fletch asked. "Tomorrow? Saturday?"

"I can't get away. I mean, two weekends in a row? I'll lose my job." Three years before, Fletch had been a member of a successful recording band. Contract with Sony Music and all. But he'd been kicked out for screwing up. Money had gone straight to his head. He'd squandered everything, common sense included, and ended up back in New Jersey as a car mechanic. Whenever he could find the time, though, he'd play pickup with local bands that needed a drummer. To earn some needed extra cash, of course, but mostly to stay young as long as he could. Next birthday he'd be twenty-six. "I'd really like to come along with you guys," he said, "but I can't afford to lose my—"

"That's okay," said Alice. "Me, Bo, and Ike, that's enough."

"Wait a second, wait a second—whoa!" Ike was swinging his head from side to side. "I'm not going anywhere. Del's not missing, she's just . . . gone."

"Yeah? What's the big difference?" said Alice. Then, "Fletch," she said, "you and Bo tell us again about this . . . guy. This guy Jude. That Del—went away with."

"I've been trying to think all week," said Fletch, "but it's like—I didn't pay too much attention. At the time. He was just some guy who showed up at both gigs."

"What about his last name?" said Alice. "Jude *what*?"

Fletch said, "I didn't hear a last name. But there *was* something funny. Funny-peculiar, I mean."

"Right!" said Bo. "I forgot!"

"What?" said Alice.

Fletch said, "He called himself—"

"The Orphan Jude," Bo finished.

2

"There were, like, four local bands played before us," said Bo. "It was supposed to be, like, twenty minutes apiece—twenty-minute sets—but these other bands all played more like half an hour. And then settin' up and gettin' off stage took—"

"Yeah, yeah, we get the picture," said Ike. "But what about this Jude? That's what we're talking about."

"I'm workin' up to it. Jeez." Bo's face reddened. "So what I'm tryin' to tell you, we were supposed to play around ten o'clock, but it was closer to, like, eleven-thirty. So we just hung around and hung around. And that's when we first seen Del talkin' to the guy. Right, Fletch?"

Fletch tilted up his coffee and swallowed the last of it. "Yeah. Right. She was hanging out with us for awhile, and then she wasn't. It got real hot and stuffy in back of the stage, so me and Bo finally went out front, and I saw Del . . ."

. . . Standing by herself, watching kids dance and then glancing up at the video monitors, which showed the same kids dancing in black and white. As always, Fletch enjoyed looking at Del. He thought he could look at her face, just *stare* at it, for hours. It wasn't that the girl was pretty; she wasn't exactly that. But she was . . . riveting.

Del had a small face, a perfect oval, and great skin except for a tiny winestain blemish, a crescent, just below the left eye. And it was a most beautiful flaw: so perfectly shaped that it might have been a two-hundred-dollar tattoo. Del, with her rust-colored hair, self-cut ragged and short; that and her slender boyish figure, a silver-gray jacket over a clean white T-shirt, dungaree coveralls, and flame-red shiny boots. Del (Just Del), she called herself. Everything combined to make her look cool and faintly ridiculous at the same time. Like some mutant in the X-Men, she had her own particular costume and her own self-invented persona.

But Fletch suspected that the real Del, Del Schofield, wasn't the one that you saw at first glance. To catch the real Del, the shy and painfully self-aware Del, you had to look at her eyes when they weren't looking back at you. . . .

"What are you thinking about?"

Fletch was startled. In the middle of the dance club, bombarded by sound, he'd drifted into reverie. And now there was Del standing beside him, smiling, her mouth and posture telescoping hip irony, but not her eyes. Not her eyes. Those looked genuinely curious.

"I was thinking," Fletch lied, "that I'm getting too old for this."

"Not you," she said. Then she looked toward the stage, at still another blasting death-metal band. All five bouncing, flailing members were dressed in red T-shirts, appliquéd with hot-rod demons. "Is there another band after this one?"

"Two more, *then* us," said Fletch. "So don't go too far."

"I'm not going anywhere." She patted his arm lightly and wandered off again.

Then Bo came over to Fletch, and they stood together. Bo kept looking around, searching for pretty southern girls, and after awhile he said, "Hey," and flicked his fingers against Fletch's arm. "Who's she talking to?"

Over there, maybe ten feet away, Del was standing with a guy who was amazingly tall and thin. He had a V-shaped head, a dead white complexion, and dark brown straight hair brushed back from a high forehead. His cheeks were hollow and his nose was long, blade-sharp. His eyes, set deep in his skull, were pouched like an insomniac's. His mouth was full-lipped and blood-red. He was dressed entirely in black. Black Cons, black jeans, black T, and a shiny black jacket with narrow lapels. . . .

*   *   *

"How old?" said Alice.

"Twenty, twenty-one, not any older," Bo said.

"Did either of you guys talk to him?"

Fletch said, "I didn't."

"I did," said Bo. "But for, like, just a second. When I went over there and told Del it was time to get ready."

"What were they talking about?"

"Shoot, *I* don't know, Alice. It was so loud in there. Del just said, 'This is Jude,' and 'This is Bo.' And that's it. Then me and Del went and got Fletch."

"That's when I asked who her new friend was," Fletch added. "And Del shrugged like he was no big deal and said he was just some guy who called himself the Orphan Jude."

"A stage name, do you think?" said Alice.

"Could be, I guess," Fletch replied.

"And, like, fifteen minutes later," said Bo, "we did our set. And we kicked butt. In, like, my humble opinion."

Alice considered. "And you saw this same guy again on Sunday?"

"At the free concert," said Fletch. "Yeah."

"And afterward, too," said Bo.

"Well, *you* saw him," said Fletch. "I didn't."

"Tell us," said Alice.

Well, the club owner knew somebody who let Del and Fletch and Bo sleep on the floor at his apartment. If they'd had to pay for motel rooms, it wouldn't have been worth the trip down there. So they crashed at this guy's place, in one of Richmond's noisier funky neighborhoods—people out in the street till four in the morning, talking and laughing and having near-homicidal family arguments.

On Sunday morning the three of them ate breakfast at a diner, then got directions to the river. There was a free concert on an island in the James, sponsored by a local radio station. You had to cross a footbridge to get there. Luckily there were stage drums that every band could use, so Fletch didn't have to lug his own kit. There were just Bo's electric bass and Del's guitar to haul.

They got there around eleven-thirty, part of a stream of people.

Because they had to drive back to Jersey that afternoon, they'd arranged to play fifth on the bill.

The first band—primitive, Straight Edge, two guys, two girls—were so inept they quit playing after the second song, and things just moved right along after that. Fletch, who'd be driving, hoped to be on the road by two-thirty or three o'clock at the latest. It seemed they were going to make it, too.

But then, ten minutes before they were supposed to play, nobody could find Del.

"I was ticked," said Fletch. "Here everything's going like clockwork, and all of a sudden Del's not around. The order had to be rearranged, and when she finally appeared, she just said she'd gone for a walk. She seemed a little . . . spacy. And when we finally were playing, I saw that guy Jude standing in the crowd."

"So you think she took a walk with *him?*" asked Alice.

"It's possible. But I don't know for sure."

"And later?" said Ike.

"Later," said Fletch, "we lugged our stuff back to the van, and we're packing everything up, and Del says, like right out of the blue, that we should go on home without her. She was gonna stay in Richmond a couple more days."

"I can't believe you just let her." Alice folded her arms irritably and gave her head a shake.

"What were we supposed to do?" said Bo. "Tie her up? She gave me her guitar, promised she'd come back on Tuesday—said she'd take the train. So what?"

"So that was a week and a half ago," said Alice.

"I know it was. That's why we're all here, isn't it? You don't have to jump down my throat. Jeez."

Alice frowned. "Bo," she said, "you saw this Jude person again—where, exactly?"

"He was sitting in a parked car across the street from the van. When we were loadin' up."

"You're sure?"

"It was him. In a big old sixties' junker. Ford, maybe."

"I didn't see anything," said Fletch.

"And then you both left."

"And then we left. That's right, Alice." Fletch picked up his empty coffee carton and fired it into the wastebasket. "You don't have to make us sound like criminals. Like I said, she's a big girl."

"She's eighteen," said Alice.

"She's twenty-one," said Ike. "What're you saying?"

"She's eighteen, which is how much you know." Alice wrinkled her forehead, then said, "All right, you guys, you can all go away now and leave me in peace. But Saturday morning, we're driving to Virginia."

"Not me," said Ike. "Just forget it. I'm not going."

Alice glared and said, "Wanna bet?"

3

By the time Alice Fuelle closed her store that evening (she'd done scarcely any business all day long), the skies had clouded over, threatening rain. A blustering, chilly wind scattered dead leaves around the sidewalk and gutters on Bowe Street, and Alice had to keep shutting her eyes against blinding grit.

As she went by the video store where Bo clerked, Alice glanced in and saw him chatting with a girl customer as they watched *Outbreak* on the monitor.

At the corner she crossed diagonally, against a red light, onto High Street.

Normally she never hurried anywhere. Alice loved the small river town on the Delaware where she'd lived all of her life and always walked around like a tourist, even in lousy weather, strolling along its crooked eighteenth-century streets, admiring the old tan brick houses that stood flush with the sidewalks. She'd even stop and read historical plaques that she knew by heart.

But that evening, cutting through the commons with its bronze war memorials (three of them), its hundred-and-fifty-year-old mulberry trees, and the ancient sycamore that marked the grave of a Leni Lenape chief, she made haste. She didn't want to be late for her consultation with Dead Mary.

"Alice!" said Danny Dunham. "Come on in. You beat the rain."

"So far," said Alice. She stepped a little hesitantly through the front door and into the boxy, low-ceilinged foyer. Facing her was the near-vertical staircase, with treads worn and

10

spongy, the risers scuffed raw. The visitors' parlor was directly to her right. To her left were dozens of small photographs in cheap gilt frames hanging on a wall. She would have had to stand in front of them to see what they were pictures of, and Alice never had the chance for that. Plus, it might have seemed nosy. She'd been inside this house only twice before, each time for a scheduled appointment. She didn't know the Dunhams socially. Nobody in town did.

Danny peered at his wristwatch. It had roman numerals and a disintegrating brown leather strap. "I'll send you up in a couple minutes," he said. "Mother told you . . . seven-fifteen, I believe?"

"Yes."

"It's not even ten past yet. Come, sit down. How about something to drink, Alice?"

"No, thank you."

She followed Danny into the parlor with upholstered furniture from sixty or seventy years ago, a green-tiled fireplace, a white mantel with beveled mirror, wine-colored drapes, and a fringed Oriental carpet. It was all maintained as immaculately as a museum display. And because of that, it was intimidating. Alice decided to stand.

But "Sit," Danny insisted and pointed to the sofa.

Taking a seat, Alice folded her hands in her lap.

As though sinking into a bathtub, Danny lowered himself slowly into a wing chair. Then he sighed. Then he crossed one leg over the other. He was at least sixty, Alice figured, and was dressed, as always, in a dark blue business suit, a white shirt, and a black-and-red tie, very shiny, with a fat and lumpy knot. Everything was rumpled or wrinkled, in need of dry cleaning. His hair, still jet black, gleamed and looked brittle from the tonic he used. Brown eyes glittered like a friendly dog's in his round, smooth face.

"Well," he said, checking his wristwatch again, "we just need to wait another minute or so. Mother can be . . . well. If I'd brought you up early—"

"It's all right, Danny," said Alice. "How's . . . how's your poetry?"

The only thing that anyone in town knew for certain about Danny Dunham was that he wrote poetry. Every day, for hours on end. But whether it was any good or not, or what it was about, or whether or not it rhymed, nobody could say, because nobody had read any of it. People said, "But wouldn't it be something if it turned out Danny Dunham was a genius—I mean, after he died. A great poet." Just the same, nobody quite believed that might be the case. And in any event, nobody quite believed Danny Dunham would ever die. Or if he did, that he would stay dead very long.

The Dunhams were one of those topics of interest—every small town has them—that get talked about several times a year at the supper table. ("I saw Danny and his mother today in the park. They're so *weird*. Pass the butter, please.")

Danny hadn't replied the first time Alice asked him about his poetry; he'd just looked at her with a shy, lopsided smile on his face. So she repeated the question.

"Still working away, yes, thank you," he said. Then he frowned heavily, his brows jutting, and looked once again at his watch. "How's . . . how's your brother?" he asked. "Computers, I think you told me once?"

"He's kind of put them behind him, I'm afraid," said Alice. "He owns his own record label now."

"Excuse me?"

"He sells records."

"I thought that's what *you* did."

"I don't mean he has a store, it's a label. He records songs and puts them out. Well—that's the *plan*, at least. He hasn't quite started yet."

"Is that something he can make a living at?"

"I hope so," said Alice, finding it curious that he would ask her such a question. After all, as far as anyone could tell, Danny Dunham had never earned so much as a dime in his life.

"I think we can go upstairs now," he said.

"Danny?" Alice had opened her leather purse and was taking out her wallet. She withdrew a ten-dollar bill.

Accepting it, and tucking it away quickly in his suit-coat pocket, Danny seemed embarrassed and avoided her eyes. He'd acted the same way about money both other times that Alice had come to see his mother.

"Shall we? . . ." he asked.

Alice followed him up the stairs and down the hall. The wallpaper, a cabbage-rose pattern, was puffed out and water-stained in several places, and the runner was threadbare. The ceiling was damaged by cracks, was missing plaster, and was crazed like old china. It seemed a different house entirely from the visitors' parlor.

Danny knocked on a bedroom door.

"Mommy? Alice Fuelle is here."

From the other side of the door came Dead Mary's querulous voice: "Well, send her in, boy!"

Shamefaced, Danny Dunham gave Alice a nod, and she opened the door.

4

"You've paid my son?"

"Yes, Mrs. Dunham."

"Have a seat, then."

Propped against several throw pillows, Dead Mary was lounging on top of her bed, which was about twice as high as the average bed, with a frame that resembled a wooden barge. She was dressed in a blue quilted robe, with pink slippers on her feet. There were magazines and newspapers splashed across her lap. Alice couldn't see any of them clearly yet, but if it was like before, they would be issues of periodicals and newspapers dating from the Second World War, or the 1950s, everything crisp and sweet with ink as though freshly printed.

A handsome but pale and fierce-looking white-haired woman, Dead Mary seemed to be seventy-five, at most. But she was much, much older. And very likely she was a ghost.

There were many people in town who swore that Mary Dunham had died of liver cancer in the early 1960s; there were some people, even, who claimed they'd gone to her funeral mass at St. Andrew's Church. But if she'd died, here she was anyhow, same as always.

And same as always, Dead Mary was still available, at a reasonable charge, to tell the future, or to find lost objects and runaway loved ones, or to carry urgent messages ("Kate is going to marry Bob Safford's grandson Mark"; "We need money") to those who'd crossed over. Who'd died, and stayed dead. Or at least stayed invisible.

Alice sat on the high-backed chair beside the bed. The way the old woman towered above her, she felt like a child.

"You've put on some weight," said Dead Mary.

"I don't think so."

"Believe me. At least five pounds. And you should eat more vegetables. You have an ugly brown streak around you."

Alice glanced down, as though expecting to see a chocolate stain on her T-shirt.

"*Around* you," said Dead Mary, frowning in irritation. "The light that surrounds you looks a little brown. Never mind." She closed the copy of *Life* magazine that she'd been reading. Clark Gable stared out from the cover. "What do you want to know, child?"

"I have this girlfriend?" said Alice, and right then Dead Mary turned to her crossly, and shook a bony finger.

"I don't wish to hear any of that lazy question-mark talk. Speak to me in complete sentences or don't speak to me at all."

Dead Mary had taught eighth grade for almost fifty years.

People in town said they bet Danny Dunham's poems were all grammatically correct.

"I'm sorry," said Alice, and started again. "My brother Ike and I met this girl named Del Schofield."

"Del? Is that shortened from Delores?"

"No, Mrs. Dunham. It's Del. Just Del. Anyhow, she didn't have a place to live, so we let her come stay with us."

"With you and your brother?"

Alice nodded. "And it turns out that Del has a great singing voice and she writes songs, and my brother recorded her a few times, right there in our house, in the kitchen actually, on some pretty cheap equipment."

"Alice. What on earth are you talking about?"

"Well, to make a long story short—"

"Please," said Dead Mary.

"Ike sent Del and a couple of musicians down to Virginia. To play at a club there, in Richmond. But then she disappeared. She told the guys—these two musicians—that she wanted to stay for a couple more days, but that was a week ago last Sunday, and we haven't heard from her since."

"And?"

"And I thought that you might be able to help me find her." From her shoulder bag, Alice took out one of Del's favorite T-shirts. That morning, she'd rolled it up into a compact tube, to make it fit. Now she unrolled it. It was black and had a huge portrait of Boris Karloff as an Egyptian mummy silkscreened on the front. Alice started to pass it to Dead Mary.

"I'm not a bloodhound! Do you have a photograph?"

"Sorry." Alice *did* have a picture, but it was in her wallet. She dug that from her bag, unsnapped the tab, and flipped through the celluloid windows, finally plucking out a trimmed color photograph of Del seated at the kitchen table, laughing.

Dead Mary cocked an eyebrow and pursed her lips when she'd had a look. "This girl," she said, "is a terrible fake."

"Excuse me?" said Alice.

"She's a fake," said Dead Mary, smiling grimly and tapping the photograph. "That smile of hers—it's all fake."

Alice was startled, but forced herself to not show it. "Anything you can tell us," she said, "to make it easier for us to find her. . . ."

She was about to say something further when she noticed that Dead Mary had closed her eyes, and that her eyelids were fidgeting.

From past experience, Alice knew it would only be a waste of breath to speak at this point.

Dead Mary had flown off to the astral plane, or whatever the heck it was that she did.

While Alice sat there waiting, steepling her fingers and tapping them together, she realized suddenly that the rain had started. It was slashing against the front windows and drumming on the roof. She got up, crossed the floor, and held back one of the fusty curtains. Outside, a branch cracked off a tree and went spinning to the pavement opposite the Dunhams' house.

As she was returning to her chair, Alice glanced toward

the bed and noticed a copy of the *Jerseyville Times* folded
lengthwise alongside Dead Mary. She picked it up. It was
dated Tuesday, November 10, 1959. The front page showed
a picture of Soviet Premier Khruschev; he was scowling and
wagging a pudgy finger in someone's face. There was a big
headline about a crisis in the Little Rock, Arkansas, public
schools, and smaller ones about Algeria, the Belgian Congo,
and new traffic lights promised for South Main Street.

Alice started paging through the newspaper, looking for
the comics, but stopped, as if commanded, when she
reached the local sports page, her attention snagged by a
photograph of Jerseyville High's varsity football team.

Standing at one end of the group—in full padded uni-
form, with his helmet wedged under his arm—was her dad,
Henry Fuelle, aged seventeen or eighteen.

At first Alice smiled, but then almost right away she
was sniffling.

She remembered her dad telling her that he'd been on
the high school football team, but she'd never seen this picture before, or any pictures from that time in his life.

After he'd graduated in 1960, he'd gone to Rutgers College, then to medical school at Johns Hopkins. He'd married
their mother—Peggy Ince from East Millstone—in 1970.
Alice was born two years later; Ike in 1975.

Driving home from Philadelphia on June 20, 1990, their
dad and mom were killed in a seven-car wreck just outside
Camden.

Carefully, Alice refolded the newspaper and placed it
back on the bed.

She used the hem of her T-shirt to blot her eyes, then
glanced over at Dead Mary, still deep in her trance.

The rain was drilling down even harder than before.

And Alice was thinking now about the first time she'd
come to see Mary Dunham. August 1990. Two months after
her parents died. She'd wanted to send them both her love
and tell them how terribly much she missed them—and to

hear something back from them, as well. If that was possible.

It was possible.

Dead Mary had reported that Alice's mom and dad weren't thrilled to be dead, but otherwise everything was okay. Being dead, they reported, was like being asleep: sometimes you dreamed, but sometimes you didn't. And of course you never woke up to eat breakfast. "And they want you to know," Dead Mary told Alice, "that they still love you. Very much. But they're worried about your brother."

Ike was fifteen at the time, irritable, sulky, and nearly always in trouble. Already he'd been arrested twice for vandalism and had been expelled for basement grades from three private high schools.

"Your folks are hoping that you'll keep a close watch on that boy," said Dead Mary.

"Tell them I will," Alice had replied. "I sure will."

The second time she went to see Dead Mary was two-and-a-half years later. Ikey had disappeared—run away—and Alice was frantic. She had no idea where he'd gone.

Dead Mary had said, "Relax, he's alive." Which was a relief. She'd also told Alice that Ike was living in New York City, washing dishes for three dollars an hour at a coffee shop, that his teeth were bothering him, that he hadn't taken a bath in weeks, that he'd started smoking cigarettes, that he'd fallen down a flight of stairs and got a nasty bruise on his shin, and that he'd probably come back home, all on his own, very shortly.

Which he had.

"Alice?"

Dead Mary's voice startled her like a sudden poke in the lower back.

"Yes?" said Alice, putting on a polite smile. But when she turned toward Dead Mary, she flinched and her smile fell.

Salmony light ran in bright, broken flickers, just as it did on theater marquees, around and around the old woman's eyelids, lips, and the rims of her ears.

A moment or two later, it vanished completely.

Lifting her head from the pillows, Dead Mary stared into Alice's face with disconcertingly green eyes. They looked troubled in a way Alice had never seen them look before.

"Don't," she said. "Please. Don't."

"Don't what?" said Alice.

"She's lost, child. You should forget about her."

"Mrs. Dunham? I'm sorry, but you're scaring me. What are you trying to tell me?"

"I'm not *trying* to tell you anything," said Dead Mary, letting her head flop down against the pillows. "I *am* telling you—don't bother with this girl. She's gone, she's lost. It's too late."

"Is she dead? Is that it?"

Dead Mary said nothing.

"Mrs. Dunham? Is my friend dead? Please tell me."

"Not dead. Lost. Gone."

"But where?"

Dead Mary raised her hands briefly, then dropped them again. "That's all I have to tell you, Alice. Please close the door firmly on your way out."

Alice blinked away black spots that fuzzed her vision, then splayed her hands on the chair arms, pushing herself to her feet. She was frightened, angry, and freezingly cold, and she felt disappointed enough to consider demanding a refund. But she kept silent. Mostly because her mouth seemed too dry to speak. She turned to go.

"Alice. Here. You forgot this."

Dead Mary was holding up the snapshot of Del.

But as Alice reached to take it, she pulled it back, holding it just out of reach. "Do you still plan on trying to find this foolish girl?"

"She's my friend!"

Dead Mary's mouth twitched at one corner. Whether it was a smile, though, or a grimace, Alice couldn't tell. "You didn't answer my question. Yes?"

"Yes," said Alice.

"Then be careful, my dear. Mind me—be very careful, indeed." She flicked the snapshot back in Alice's direction.

Alice took it, put it away, said good night, and shut the door behind her. In a kind of daze, she walked down the stairs to the foyer. "Danny?" she called. "I'm going home now. Thank you. Danny?"

He didn't reappear; she could hear him typing, somewhere.

With a shrug, Alice reached for the front door, then hesitated. She turned around, glancing into the visitors' parlor and up the staircase, then she tiptoed over and looked at the framed photographs hanging on the opposite wall.

Some were black-and-white and deckle-edged, others in glossy color; some faded, milky Polaroids. She recognized several of the people in them—people she'd seen around town. Many of them—Mr. Crumley the pharmacist, old Mrs. Gomer, Mrs. Hokanson, Mr. and Mrs. Dillon, a lawyer on crutches named Joe Mosley, and Dr. Gleason—were dead.

A picture of her parents was hanging up there, too.

So was a picture of her brother, Ike.

Alice knew both those pictures well: they were in a family photo album that she'd put together herself.

Slowly, trembling slightly, she lifted a hand to her mouth.

But it dropped like a lump of lead when she saw the final picture on the lefthand side, bottom row.

Del Schofield laughing in Alice's kitchen. But it couldn't be!

Alice slung her bag down on the hall table, scrabbled through it, grabbed her wallet and snapped it open.

She flicked, clumsy-fingered, through the windows.

Del's picture wasn't in there.

Instead, where it should have been, where she had just put it a minute ago, was a photo Alice had never seen before.

It was a color picture of a white canvas wall tent, staked in the middle of an attic floor. You could see rafters, cobwebs, and glints of daylight leaking through chinks in old clapboard. There was a small medallion window.

Be careful, said Dead Mary, in Alice's head. *Be very careful.*

5

Supper, for the second time that week, was going to be pancakes and apple sauce—because that's what Ike felt like preparing. He knew Alice would roll her eyes, but she wouldn't say anything snotty. She really didn't care what she ate. Alice ate to live. Period. Same as Ike. It wasn't that he especially *craved* pancakes tonight; they were just easy to prepare. You mixed everything in the same bowl, and there was only one frying pan. Not much to clean up.

As he was getting two eggs off the refrigerator door, Ike suddenly thought about Del Schofield.

When she was living there in the house and it was pancakes for supper, she preferred grape jelly to maple syrup and sprinkled cinnamon on her apple sauce.

He remembered that now and thought how Del looked sitting opposite him at the kitchen table, her small pale face bent to her plate, her hair sticking up in twenty crazy directions. She always ate quickly and smiled like a prizewinner when she finished.

He was still thinking about Del while he poured pancake mix into a yellow bowl—not bothering to measure, just pouring—and then cracked in the eggs, slopped in the milk, then a little canola oil. He was thinking—remembering—that Del drank three cups of coffee every night after supper. But she never wanted dessert. No, wait, that wasn't entirely true. She liked ice cream, but only if there weren't nuts in it. Her favorite was mint chocolate chip.

Whisking the batter, Ike decided that it was too quiet in the kitchen—in the house—so he switched on the radio, spinning the tuner and creating a blat of sound till he pulled in, though just barely, a local college station. In the middle of a crash tune by a band called Framed Art.

Framed Art. They used to be called Suzi Boy. Ike had heard them play in New Brunswick early the previous summer, and tried to interest them in recording something for his fledgling label. They'd talked to him, seemed interested, but finally couldn't wait for him to get set up properly, and they had signed with another indie. And now here they were, four months later, calling themselves Framed Art, with an EP out and getting college airplay.

If Del wasn't such an irresponsible loser, such a jerk, she could have had the same thing by January at the latest. Ike had promised her. He had the money to book studio time in Trenton; he was going to go directly to CD—order two thousand units with a classy two-color insert. He'd *promised* her.

Del had always looked so amused whenever he started raving about his big plans. "You gonna make me a star?" she'd say, with a quirk of her little red mouth.

"That's exactly what I'm gonna do," Ike told her a dozen times. "And then I'm gonna sell your contract in a year, maybe less, to a major label—and then I'm gonna retire. Be rich and retire."

"And do what?" Del would ask.

Whatever I want to do, Ike thought now. Whatever I want to do. Whatever *that* is.

He rinsed the whisk under the faucet, covered the pancake batter, and set the mixing bowl aside.

Then he sat down to wait for Alice to come home.

He listened to the radio.

Half-listened.

And finally he wasn't listening at all.

Abruptly, Ike stood up and left the kitchen, walked down the short hall, then turned into the little sewing room they'd let Del use for a bedroom since the middle of July.

He looked slowly around at her posters, his gaze moving

from Evan Dando to Michael Stipe to Chrissie Hynde to Beck, then he frowned and sat down on her bed.

A copy of *Betty and Veronica* lay facedown on the pillow.

Smiling, Ike picked up the comic book and flipped through it, thinking about the first time he'd seen Del. On July 7, last summer. On the towpath of the old canal that cut through town.

Hands in his pockets, ideas flopping around in his head like caught fish, Ike was out walking that morning. He'd only recently decided to launch his own label and was trying to figure out what to do first. All he'd really need was a couple of thousand dollars, maybe not even that. And he was pretty sure that he could get a loan from Alice. She'd been pushing him hard ever since he'd quit college to find something to do with his life; so money wouldn't be any major problem.

No, the problem was finding a good band.

Lately he'd been hanging out at small music clubs in North Jersey, Philly, and New York City, seeing which bands drew crowds and compiling a list of possibles.

The thing was, Ike Fuelle wanted to hit it big, strike it rich, the first time out. He had to be very careful—had to pick a band that was going to be the next R.E.M., the next Pearl Jam or Smashing Pumpkins. He wasn't going into this business just for the fun of it, or even because he especially liked music. (In fact, he didn't—not especially.) He was going into it strictly to make a lot of money, fast. So that he could retire at twenty-one.

And then do, for the rest of his life, whatever he wanted.

Whatever *that* was.

So there was Ike scuffling along the towpath, jays screeching in the trees and midges whirling around his head. Then he saw her.

A skinny girl with jagged-cut red hair, pale skin, a small hooked nose, dark glasses, and a slender, crescent-shaped birthmark on her left cheek. On the back of her white T-shirt, Godzilla trampled Tokyo.

She was perched on an old limestone mile-marker reading a comic book.

On the ground beside her lay a bulging knapsack, a bedroll, a pair of sneakers, and a big guitar—an acoustic-electric—with ornate fretwork against dark wood.

She'd looked around when she heard him—peering at Ike casually over a shoulder, not startled. Then she nodded and went back to reading her comic book.

It was a *Betty and Veronica*.

Ike passed her by with just the merest glance. They didn't speak a word.

He continued walking for another ten or fifteen minutes, finally stopping at a wooden bridge that spanned the canal. He climbed onto the railing, then—dangling his legs and looking at his reflection squiggle in the green water below—he tried to dream up a good name for his label. How 'bout . . . Rocket Fuelle Records? Or was that too corny?

He couldn't think of anything else, anything better, so he gave it up after a while and started back to town.

It was close to noon by then, and the daylight had changed, grown stronger and a brighter yellow. When he came upon that girl again, Ike was amazed. She looked positively golden, sitting in an overhead shaft of light that broke through the foliage. She glowed, or seemed to. Man, she looked . . . dramatic. Like a punk saint.

She'd put aside her comic book and had her guitar resting across her knees, using it as a portable desk. A piece of paper was smoothed out on the guitar body, and she was writing something with a pencil stub.

Ike said, "Hey," and she glanced up.

"Hey," she replied.

Then Ike took a chance, pushing it. What the hell.

He asked her what she was writing.

Her eyes squinted and her mouth turned up in a half-smile.

"Shopping list," she replied with a mocking smile. Then she laughed, looking back at her piece of paper and pre-

tending to read: "Fruit juice. Rice cakes. Peanut butter. Um—soda. Donuts. Powdered *and* chocolate. And a table to eat everything at. A kitchen for the table. A house for the kitchen. A great *big* house. For my million friends. Lots of land. A swimming pool. A stable. Ten, twelve horses. And . . . that's it!" She laughed again, then crumpled up the paper and stuffed it into her pocket.

Ike cocked an eyebrow. He hadn't expected her voice to be husky. He'd expected it to be small and thin, like her. But it was deep and way husky. Don't get excited, he thought. She probably can't sing.

Even so, he was on the verge of asking if she could play that guitar when the girl suddenly stood up and leaned it against the mile-marker. She looked him over with a cool appraising gaze that Ike found unsettling.

"Are you walking back to town?" she said.

"Yeah."

"Well, don't let me keep you."

She stood there waiting for him to leave, and he finally did, almost certain that behind his back she was smirking.

It was crazy, but Ike suddenly had this freshman-in-high-school impulse to turn around, go charging back, and push her into the canal. . . .

Now, in Del's bedroom, he reached over and picked up her comic book. He rolled it into a tube, squeezed the tube in his fist, pressed it against his forehead, and then closed his eyes.

Where the hell *was* she?

As Ike stood to go, he glanced at the dresser. He walked over to touch the neck of Del's guitar, running his thumb down its strings, plucking each one.

I miss you, he thought.

He'd never tell his sister—never!—but he missed Del Schofield something awful. And he was worried about her.

Worried sick.

6

Five seconds after she'd left Dead Mary's house and stepped into the roaring downpour, Alice Fuelle was drenched. But she hardly noticed.

She was thinking about that photograph in her wallet.

"Alice, for crying out loud—climb in!"

The command was punctuated by a loud horn blast.

Finally, Alice looked up, looked around, and looked through the rain curtain. There was Fletch—in greasy coveralls and a cap—hanging out the driver's door of a tow truck, gesturing for her to come around and jump in. "Girl, you want an engraved invitation?"

"No, that's quite all right," she said and laughed.

"I must've beeped ten times."

"I'm sorry," she said, getting in. "This is really nice—thanks, Fletch. What a night."

"No kidding." He put the truck back into gear, gave it some gas, and steered away from the curb.

The wipers thumped. Rain crashed on the cab roof.

As Alice pushed wet hair back from her face, she realized Fletch was playing a dub of the tape that Del Schofield had recorded in her kitchen last month.

It was the song called "You Never Heard of Where I Come From."

She smiled, listening to Del's raspy voice, the slow cadence of minor chords, and Ike's thudding, erratic percussion—he'd used a wooden spoon on the stove burners.

"She's good, isn't she?" said Alice.

"She's not bad," Fletch replied. "But your brother stinks." Then he glanced over and said, "Yeah, she's good. Real good. People liked her down in Richmond. She was kind of stiff

27

and all, and she never spoke a word at the mike, just sang. But people liked her."

Alice nodded. "I thought they would. Ike did, too."

"So how come he didn't come down with us? I know what he said about hating long drives, but why didn't he come down with us, really?"

"I think he was afraid."

"Of what?"

"I don't know for sure. He's funny that way. I think he was even more nervous about it than Del."

"She didn't seem nervous to me."

"Yeah? Well, she can pretend pretty good. She was scared out of her mind," said Alice.

"You think she might've just run away 'cause she didn't want to do it anymore?"

"Do what anymore, sing? No. You said she was excited, right? After both performances."

"I did. But she can pretend pretty good—isn't that what you just told me?"

Alice shook her head. "If she was gonna take off, she never would've given you guys her guitar. No way. Plus, she left all of her stuff at my house. All her comic books and her books about magic. All her T-shirts. No, she meant to come back. I know she did. I just wish I knew why she stayed down there in the first place."

"That guy Jude," said Fletch.

"Yeah," said Alice. "Him again."

"Hey, Alice?"

"Hmmm?"

"What do you know about Del?"

"For sure? Not much. She told me and Ike that she grew up in Milwaukee."

"Funny—she told me Seattle."

Alice half-turned in her seat and looked at Fletch.

"And she told Bo," said Fletch, "that she came from Detroit. And she told Ike that she was twenty-one."

"And me that she was eighteen," said Alice, nodding. "Yeah, I guess she has a very creative mind."

"That's one way of putting it," said Fletch. Then he suddenly reached and ejected the cassette. "How'd you and your brother ever get hooked up with her? He find her in a club?"

"You never heard? No, he just met her one morning out on the canal. And later that same day? She walked into my store lugging her stuff. Dumped it all right on the floor, then spent the next two hours sitting at the boom-box, listening to CDs with the headphones on. She looked so skinny."

"And what happened next?" Fletch laughed. "Wait, don't tell me: You took her home for supper."

Alice stared through the windshield.

"You did, didn't you? Good old Alice and her heart of gold." He poked her in the ribs with his index finger. She whacked it away, but laughed despite herself.

"It wasn't *just* because she looked half-starved," Alice said a few moments later. "It was . . . I thought we'd maybe have a lot in common."

"Looking for a friend, huh?"

"What's wrong with that?"

"Nothing, Alice, nothing. But so what made you think you guys had stuff in common? 'Cause you liked the same music?"

"That, and—other things." Alice thought for a moment. "She lost her parents, too. Like me and Ikey did."

"Yeah, so where'd she lose 'em?" said Fletch. "In Milwaukee? Seattle? Or Detroit?"

Alice flared. "She wasn't lying about that! No. She wouldn't."

"Why not?"

"She just . . . wouldn't. All right?"

Fletch had turned into Farragut Street and now pulled the truck to the curb in front of Alice's little clapboard house.

"I appreciate the ride," she said curtly.

"Look at me, Alice. Don't be mad, okay? I'm not trying to make Del look bad, I'm just trying to . . . to figure the girl out."

29

"I know. And I'm not mad. But she really *is* an orphan."

"Like you," said Fletch.

"Like me and Ike, yeah."

"And Jude."

Alice flinched. Then, wide-eyed, she stared at Fletch. "What're you *saying*?"

"Nothing. Absolutely nothing. 'Cept that it's a pretty funny coincidence."

"Something's wrong, Fletch. I know it. Something bad."

He focused on her completely. "What did Dead Mary say?"

Alice pretended surprise.

"I saw you come out of there," said Fletch. "What did she tell you?"

"That I should just forget about Del. That she's . . . lost. But what *that* means, I don't—"

Making a snap decision, Alice opened her bag, dug out her wallet, and showed Fletch the picture of the white tent.

He reached up and switched on the overhead light.

"That's where she is," said Alice. "Maybe. I don't know."

"Where did you get this?"

Alice said nothing.

"From Mary Dunham?"

She nodded.

Fletch studied the photograph again.

"I don't get it."

"Neither do I."

Fletch sucked on his front teeth, making a sizzling hot-oil sound. "I'm going down there with you guys. Back to Richmond."

"I thought you had to work."

"I'm coming with you."

Alice smiled, leaned over, tipped up his chin with her fingertip, and kissed him on the cheek.

"We're leaving early Saturday—around eight? From my house."

Fletch took one final glance at the photograph. "I'll be there," he promised.

7

By noontime the following Saturday—a bright, warm, and diamond-clear day—they'd already passed Baltimore and were coming up on Washington, D.C. "So what do you figure?" said Alice, who was driving. "Get there by, when? Two? Two-thirty?"

"I guess," said Fletch. "That sounds about right."

Bo said, "Just don't speed, okay? We got a ticket last time right around here. It's in the glove compartment."

"Oh, thanks a lot," said Alice. "Thanks a bunch. You guys are paying."

"That was cute, huh, Bo?" said Fletch, and the two of them, sitting in the rear of the van, cracked up.

Ike, riding shotgun, twisted around and looked back at them. "What's so funny about a speeding ticket?"

"We didn't tell you?" said Fletch. "About Del's magic trick?"

"Her spell," said Bo. "Del's spell!" He burst out laughing again.

"What?" asked Alice.

"You know that goofy book she got? What's it called?"

"Practical Magic?" said Alice.

"That's it! That's the one. Did you ever look at it? It's a riot," said Fletch. "Tells you how to cast all these dippy spells with, like, ordinary stuff you can find around the house. For people who can't get their hands on newt blood and wing of bat and eye of toad. You ever see it?"

"We've seen it," said Ike, scowling. "So what happened?"

"So Del finds a magic recipe in there that's supposed to make it so you don't get any traffic tickets."

"You're kidding!" said Alice.

"No, I swear. Right, Bo? And what you're supposed to do, according to this book? You put a used Kleenex, it's gotta be crusty—"

"Oh, gross!" said Ike.

"A crusty Kleenex, and some fingernail clippings from everybody who's riding in the car—"

"You're making this up," said Alice.

"Swear to God, it's all in that goofy book. Fingernail clippings, and that tissue, and a piece of paper with your license plate number written on it. And then you put everything into the ashtray."

"Yeah?" said Ike. "And? *And?* . . ."

"Well," Bo said, "you don't do anything till you see a cop car behind you with the flasher going. Soon as you do, you're supposed to light the piece of paper and the crusty tissue. And then, according to Del's book, the cop is bound to change his mind and go after somebody else. Only that's not what happened."

"Obviously," said Alice. "But so what *did* happen?"

"State cop pulls us over, walks up to the van, and what's he see, first thing? A fire in the ashtray." Fletch chuckled. "Naturally, he figures we're burning something illegal, something we don't want *him* to find—so he makes us all get out, and I thought we were gonna get busted for sure."

"For crying out loud," said Alice. "You're serious? This really happened?"

" 'Fraid so," said Fletch. "But at least we got off with just a speeding ticket."

"That stupid book," said Bo. "I was ready to throw it out the window. Where the heck did she ever get that stupid thing?"

Alice said, "At a tag sale. She loves it. But I never thought that she—*believed* in any of it. I thought it was just something to goof on."

"That's how much *you* know about Del," said Ike.

Quickly, Alice turned her head and looked at him. "What's that supposed to mean?"

32

"Nothing. Forget it."

"No—what?"

"Forget it," said Ike. "Nothing." He slumped against the door, his cheek to the glass, and slowly let his vision unfocus until the trees along the highway became a flickering smear.

In his mind's eye he was seeing, with crystal clarity, three green taper candles, each one burning in a small juice glass. Sprinkled around the glasses, in helical patterns on the tabletop, were caraway seeds and cumin seeds, peppercorns, oregano flakes, soap shavings, match tips, and cigarette tobacco. . . .

It had been a month ago. Ike was in his bedroom, way late, poring over catalogs from several different record plants, comparing their prices. How much for so many chrome cassettes, so many seven-inch vinyls, so many CDs. The greater the volume, the less the unit cost. And blah-blah-blah. His mind boggled at so much arithmetic. He had a calculator on the desk and was tapping out sums. Jotting figures on a pad, scratching them out—then starting over again. Over and over again. He finally pushed his chair away from the desk and stood up, stretching.

He was dead tired, but excited, too.

This crazy idea that he'd had, starting his own record company, suddenly it wasn't so crazy.

Not since Del Schofield had arrived.

Amazing! Ike still couldn't believe it. There he'd been scouting every place he knew for a decent band, and who shows up one summer's day, out of the clear blue sky, but this bizarro girl with a great big voice. Who could play guitar. And write her own songs. *Good* songs, too. Quirky and dark, with strong hooks, and melodies that snagged in your head.

Whenever Ike thought about it, he got a little scared. He wasn't used to lucky breaks. You could say that again. In fact, he was used to the exact opposite. To crummy luck. Anything that he'd ever tried to do, or wished he could be good at, had been a total fiasco. Examples? All right. He'd gone to New York City to become an actor. Signed up for an acting class and was laughed out of it in two weeks flat. No talent. He'd tried to write short stories, and they'd bored even *him* to death. No talent. He'd tried to learn about computers, figuring he could make a lot of money designing games, but was utterly flummoxed by C++. No talent. No aptitude. No nothing. Nada.

And he'd lasted a mere three-and-a-half weeks in a community college.

Up till now, Ike Fuelle hadn't found a thing that he could do well. Except gripe and act gloomy to his sister and everybody else in the world.

Deep gloom and chronic griping were excellent armor.

But this music idea: well, now. He just might, at last, have found his niche.

A niche.

A niche to make him wealthy.

And once he was rolling in money, *then* he could figure out what he *really* wanted to do.

Yeah, this nutty scheme, this Ike-Fuelle-the-music-industry-mogul crazy idea, didn't seem at all nutty or crazy anymore. Or stupid, or hopeless. Or doomed.

Thanks to Del Schofield.

Who'd dropped, like a gift, into Ike's nowhere-and-nothing-special life.

For the first time since his parents had died and his world had turned upside-down, Ike felt good about himself. And hopeful.

Thanks to Del.

Naturally, though, he wasn't going to let anybody *know* how keenly hopeful and good he felt.

They'd laugh, most likely. Think he'd gone all soft and goofy.

If you looked angry all the time, people respected you.

Of course, they didn't much *like* you, either. But Ike could live with that.

After the crick was out of his neck, he put away his calculator, his catalogs, and his scratch paper. Time for bed.

But, no big surprise, he couldn't sleep. Instead, he just tossed and turned, his mind busy—teeming—with ideas. He'd make dubs of Del's kitchen tapes, send them around. To radio stations. College stations. And try to get her some gigs. She needed a stage act. Whoa, he thought. Wait a second. There was a guy he'd met in New York named Mouse, Mouse Mineo, who'd been the assistant night manager at the Hard Rock Cafe on Fifty-Seventh Street. Last that Ike had heard, Mouse had moved to Virginia, started his own little music club down there. But where? Norfolk? Was it Norfolk? No, hold on. Richmond.

It was Richmond. Mouse Mineo was in Richmond!

Ike jumped out of bed, snapped on a light, grabbed a Magic Marker and printed himself a big note—CALL MOUSE—on a piece of paper, which he then taped to his desk lamp. So he'd spot it first thing in the morning.

And then he went back to bed. For another sleepless half-hour.

Screw it, he thought, and got dressed again and went downstairs, intending to pour himself a bowl of Cheerios and watch some TV.

He walked into the kitchen and stopped dead.

There was Del, seated at the table, candlelight scribbling her small narrow face with quick shadows and light.

And three green taper candles, each one burning in a juice glass.

Sprinkled around the glasses, in spiral patterns on the tabletop, were caraway seeds and cumin seeds, peppercorns, oregano flakes, soap shavings, match tips, and cigarette tobacco.

"Hey, sit down." She used her foot to shove a chair away from the table. "You're just in time. I'm trying to conjure an imp," she said. "To do my bidding. But you can have dibs on him, too," she continued. "If you're nice."

"A what?" said Ike. "You're trying to conjure a *what*?"

35

"An imp," Del said, pointing to her book of magic spells, the one she'd bought a few days earlier for two bucks.

"What's an imp?" Ike felt like he was talking to a child. Or a deranged person.

"I don't know," said Del. "But it says here if you get one to come? He'll take you anyplace you want to go."

Ike said, "Uh-huh. And where do you wanna go?"

"I don't really care," said Del. "So long as it's empty."

"Empty?"

"With nobody around," she said. " 'Cause then I wouldn't have to feel guilty for being lonesome. 'Cause if there's nobody else around, hey, it's not your fault if you're lonesome—right?" Then she quickly added, "Sit down, Ike, sit down. But don't make any sudden movements. Got it? We don't want to scare away the imp."

Ike said, "You feel . . . lonesome?"

It was an odd, dizzying moment for Ike Fuelle. How can she be lonesome? he thought. She's got us. She's got Alice. And me. She's got me and Alice. And me.

He felt disappointed and crestfallen and painfully unhappy, all at once.

And seeing Del staring so intently at the candle flames, he also felt frightened.

Who *was* this girl, really? This girl who wore horror-movie T-shirts and read *Betty and Veronica* comic books, who played guitar and wrote strange, haunted songs, who tried to conjure up magic imps at two in the morning with candles, tobacco, soap flakes, and kitchen spices?

Who smiled all the time, but claimed she was lonesome.

Who *was* she, really?

Ike had no idea. That much was certain.

But he didn't want her to be lonesome.

That he knew—starkly and suddenly—for absolute sure.

"Del? . . ."

"Shhhhh. Sit down if you're gonna sit down. But don't talk."

Ike remained standing by the table for several more seconds. Then he turned around and walked out.

And since Del Schofield was still there the following morning, he figured that no imp had materialized.

Thank God. . . .

"Ikey?"

"Huh?"

"You all right?"

"Yeah, sure. Why?"

"You haven't said anything for an hour," said Alice. "That's why."

"I'm fine," said Ike. "I'm . . . fine."

"Almost there!" Bo yelled from the back of the van, as they passed a sign for Richmond.

Twenty-five miles to go.

Twenty-five miles to go. But *then* what?

8

Without gel-lights, noise, loud music, and a couple of hundred kids, the Moon Lamp was only a shabby cavern with spooky acoustics. And Ike Fuelle found nothing more dispiriting than a dance club in the daytime.

It was now half-past three that Saturday afternoon.

"You come down by yourself?" asked Mouse Mineo.

"Huh? No," said Ike. "No, my sister's with me. And those two guys who played with Del—you must've met 'em."

"Uh-huh," said Mouse.

"I had 'em drop me off. They're parking the van. They'll be along any minute."

Mouse said, "Uh-huh." He was a short, wiry guy in his mid-twenties with greasy long black hair, pinched features, a ghostly complexion—almost a prison pallor—and dark wet eyes. He wore five stud earrings in each ear. Heavy coil rings on spidery fingers. As he sat beside Ike at the juice bar in his empty club, he kept taking the rings off and putting them back on, though on different fingers every time. He was wearing a jean jacket over a purple T-shirt screened with the club's logo, tight jeans, and badly scuffed suede boots.

"Uh-huh," said Mouse for maybe the twentieth time in the past ten minutes. When Ike knew him back in New York City, he'd been the same way. Never much of a talker. "So?"

"So, like I said, I'm wondering if you seen Del again."

"After the night she was here, you mean? Nope." Mouse grinned suddenly, revealing sharp yellow canine teeth. "So what're you *now*, Ike—a private detective? Actor, computer genius, music producer . . . private detective?"

Ike felt himself blush and hated it.

"I'm just trying to find her, Mouse. Actually—personally—I don't give a damn. It's my sister's big idea."

"Uh-huh." Mouse pulled off two rings and replaced them on his fingers in reverse positions. "So you're still a music producer."

"Absolutely."

"Any product yet?"

"Soon," said Ike.

"Uh-huh. Well, let me tell you something, guy. Find Del."

Ike stared at him blankly.

"What I'm saying is, the girl's good. Find her, get her in a studio. Or somebody else is gonna, guaranteed."

Ike folded his arms across his chest and nodded, feeling complimented. "Didn't I tell you she was good? You could hear that even on that demo I sent you, right?"

"Speaking of that. Whoever did the percussion? Bag him. Crying out loud, guy nearly ruined her songs."

"Yeah, well, he's long gone. Yeah, I know. But Del, *she's* the real thing—like I told you. Right?"

Mouse said, "Uh-huh," then glanced behind him at the sound of a door opening. He lifted an arm casually and waved. "Your sister?"

Ike looked. "Yeah." Alice, standing framed in a rectangle of daylight, wiggled her fingers. "Alice," he called, "I'll be with you in a minute. Whyn't you and the guys go grab a cup of coffee?"

Even from across the dance floor, he could see the frown of irritation appear on her face. But she didn't give him any grief, merely nodded and went back outside, closing the door behind her.

"Cute," said Mouse.

"Who? My sister?"

Mouse laughed. "Yeah. Your sister."

"I guess," said Ike with a little shrug. Then he said, "It was all her idea, coming down here looking for Del."

"Smart idea," said Mouse.

Ike cocked his head, pretending to consider, then nodded.

"Only we got no idea where Del's been for the past two weeks."

"I'll ask around tonight."

"Would you? Thanks, Mouse." Then he said, "And this guy I described to you—all dressed in black? This Jude guy. Ring a bell?"

Mouse shook his head, grinning again. "Half the guys comin' in here look like that. I don't pay much attention. Too busy, you know?"

"There's not a band or anything, is there? Called The Orphan Jude? Or Jude the Orphan? Anything like that?"

"Not that I ever heard." Mouse swiveled around on his stool to face Ike. "You going to the police?"

"Jeez, I don't know. She's a missing person, I guess. But Del's *always* been a missing person."

Mouse tipped his chin up, meaning, Say what?

"She's a drifter. At least that's what she told me and Alice."

"Drifter shmifter," said Mouse. "Maybe she puts on a good enough act, but it's not a great act, know what I mean? She's no drifter. Get real, Ike. Bet you anything she's from the 'burbs of Jersey."

Ike gave a half-shrug.

"Go to the cops," said Mouse. "You got a picture to show them?"

"Sure."

"Got a picture to show me?"

Ike said yeah, and got his wallet out, then passed Mouse a color snapshot. It was one from the roll of thirty-six that he'd taken of Del just three weeks earlier, hoping to get a CD cover out of it.

In the picture, Del had on a *Clockwork Orange* T-shirt— a derbied Malcolm McDowell brandishing a stiletto and leering like a psychopath.

Del herself was smiling, though. Sweetly.

"I'll show this around," said Mouse.

"That'd be cool. I'll check back with you. Or you can give me a call. We're staying at the Holiday Inn."

Ike dropped off his barstool and shook hands with Mouse.

As he was crossing the dance floor to go out, he stopped, glanced over at the small bandstand, smiled, then turned back around. Mouse was watching him.

"She really *is* good, isn't she?"

"How come you didn't come down to watch her play?"

"Ah, you know," said Ike. " 'Fraid I'd make her nervous. Being her manager and all."

Mouse laughed and shook his head. "See ya, Ike."

"Yeah."

"Ikester!"

"Yeah?"

"When you find her? You'd best lock her in a studio, first thing. That way, you just might make something out of your sorry self."

Ike scowled, waved briefly, then opened the door.

When I find her? he thought.

If.

9

When Ike Fuelle stepped out of the Moon Lamp into late afternoon sunlight, it nearly blinded him. He lifted a hand and shaded his eyes. Then he looked around, up and down the sidewalk. Where were the others? Directly next door to the club was a junk store with old percolators and waffle irons and thermos jugs and board games and *National Geographic*s jumbled together in plastic milk crates on the pavement out in front. Standing at the open front door, an old man with fluffy white hair said hello. Ike nodded and started walking up the block, passing a hardware store, then an empty store, then stopping to look through a restaurant window. Where was Alice?

"We were gonna let you wander around for a while," said Bo, suddenly appearing in back of Ike and tapping him on the arm. "But Fletch said that was kind of stupid."

"Good for Fletch," said Ike.

"We're across the street." Bo pointed to a luncheonette with a huge round, faded-to-pink Coca-Cola sign over the door. "Alice is mad at you."

"For what?" said Ike, though he already knew the answer.

" 'Cause you didn't let her come into the club. 'Cause you didn't introduce her to Mouse. And 'cause you're acting like a big twit again. Hey, don't look at *me*. That's her talking."

When Ike and Bo came into the luncheonette, Alice and Fletch were sitting at a round window table writing some kind of list. Most of the other tables were unoccupied, but several middle-aged men in plaid shirts were seated on red-topped stools at the counter. A country song sugared up with violins played from an old jukebox that looked like Robbie the Robot. The air was a little bit smoky. Griddle smoke and cigarette smoke. Somewhere, toast popped with a metallic *jinng*!

Alice didn't look up when Ike sat down beside her. Yeah, she was mad at him, all right. Well, maybe not exactly mad. Her feelings were hurt. Ike decided he could live with that.

"So?" she asked, still not looking at him. "What did you find out?" On the piece of paper in front of her, she quickly numbered several items with a pencil. 1, 2, 3, 4. "You find out anything useful, Sherlock?"

"Whyn't you shut up?" said Ike. He reached over and picked up Alice's Coke—in a tall, red plastic tumbler, with lots of ice—and took a sip. Not from her straw, though.

"We're waiting," said Alice.

Fletch quirked his mouth sideways and rolled his eyes.

"Mouse hasn't seen Del since the night she played there. She hasn't been back," Ike said. "And this Jude person doesn't ring a bell with him." He pointed to the paper lying on the table in front of Alice. "What're you doing?"

"Making a list," she replied coolly. "So we can do things in an organized manner."

Ike covered his smirk with a hand. *Do things in an organized manner.* That was Alice for you. She *always* did things in a freaking organized manner. It drove Ike nuts. He reached for the list, but she snatched it away.

"How y'all doin' here?"

A young waitress (first things you noticed: her flyaway black hair, her green eyes) had come by—sort of drifted lazily over—and stood now at Ike's right shoulder. She was thin and very tall with straight, narrow hips and long, skinny legs. "How 'bout you?" she said to Ike. "Get you something to drink?"

"Coffee," Ike replied. "No, make it a Coke. Thanks."

"Fill that up for you?" the waitress asked Bo, pointing at his tumbler.

Bo didn't answer: he was staring intently at her face with his mouth open.

"Yeah, he'll have another," Alice finally answered for him. "And nothing else for me."

"Or me," said Fletch.

The waitress nodded, smiled, and went away.

As soon as she did, Bo leaned forward, elbows on the tabletop. "You hear that?" he said eagerly. "She said 'you-all.' You hear that?" He beamed. " 'How *you-all* doin' here?' I love that! They really say stuff like that!"

Alice glowered. "Can we get back to business?"

"Sure, sure," said Bo, but he slung an arm along the back of his chair and gazed across the luncheonette at the waitress. "How old d'you figure she is? You think she's our age, don't you, Ike?"

"Come on, man," said Fletch. "Get serious, all right? We're down here to find Del."

"Thank you, Fletch," said Alice.

Ike noticed the grateful smile accompanying her words. It looked a bit wider and several degrees warmer than necessary. Almost . . . flirty.

Oh, great, he thought.

"Here's what me and Fletch think we should do," said Alice, tapping the sheet of paper with an index finger. "First—well, the first thing was talk to Mouse Mineo. We already did that."

"*I* already did that," said Ike.

She gave him a sour look and struck off number one with her pencil.

"Next," she said, "Fletch and me thought we should go to a quick-print place, see if we can run off a bunch of flyers."

"Maybe even put Del's picture on it," Fletch added, "if it doesn't cost too much. And then we can go around handing them out, putting them on lampposts, that kind of thing. And then go back to the Moon Lamp tonight, to show 'em around there."

"And number three?" asked Ike.

The waitress came back and set down Ike's Coke and Bo's

iced tea. She lifted an eyebrow slightly when she heard Alice say, "Number three? Go to the police."

Bo turned to the waitress. "You know where police headquarters is, darlin'?"

He'd never said "darlin'" before in his entire life. But what the heck, he figured. He was in Richmond, Virginia; he was in the South. People said "darlin'" here all the time, didn't they?

The waitress looked at Bo and laughed. "I sho 'nuff do, honey chile," she said, clearly goofing, and Bo's face turned a dark pomegranate red.

"Excuse him, please," said Alice. "He's a bit of a nitwit."

"Oh, that's all right," the waitress said. "Where are you guys from?"

"New Jersey."

"Yeah? I'm from New York. Upstate. Around Albany." She turned and smiled at Bo. "I've been here a few years, though. *Darlin'.*"

Bo's toothy grin froze on his face.

"Police headquarters," the waitress went on, "is up by the State Capitol and City Hall. Maybe four or five blocks."

"So what's number four on the list?" said Ike after the waitress had gone back to the counter.

"It's a long shot," said Alice, then she hesitated and glanced sidelong at Fletch. He nodded. "But somebody should go check out a few sporting-goods stores."

Ike was astonished. "*Sporting*-goods stores? What for?"

"There's something that I haven't told you," Alice said. "Or Bo."

Ike looked at Fletch. And thought, But him you *did* tell? "What?" he asked.

Taking out her wallet, Alice carefully removed the photograph—a white wall tent pitched in an attic room—and laid it on the table.

"We ought to see if anybody recognizes a tent like this one."

45

Ike folded his arms across his chest, waiting for the explanation.

When he finally received it, he couldn't stop shaking his head. "Why didn't you *tell* me you went and saw Dead Mary?"

" 'Cause you'd just make fun. You don't believe in her."

"She's a big phony."

"There! That's how come I didn't tell you, Ikey."

"Ike. *Ike!*"

"That's why I didn't tell you . . . Ike. But *you* tell *me* this: How did this picture get into my wallet?"

"Her stupid son put it there when your back was turned."

"No way!"

"All right. For the moment, let's just say it *is* magic. Or whatever. So? What's it supposed to *mean?*" said Ike. "Picture of a tent—what's *that* supposed to mean?"

"I don't know. Yet."

"Yet," said Ike with taunting sarcasm.

"Lay off," snapped Fletch. "I'm getting sick and tired of you, you know that?"

"I care? Do I look like I care?"

"Enough!" said Alice, and she hit the table with the flat of her hand. "You don't have to go check on any tents if you don't want to, Ike. Okay? You don't believe it's anything, fine. Bo can do it. All right, Bo?"

"Yeah. I guess."

"And Fletch can see about getting some flyers made. And I'll go talk to the police."

Ike lifted one hand and let it drop. "And what am I supposed to do?"

Fletch said, "You can stick your thumb up your—"

"Quit it," Alice said. "Ike can come with me, if he wants."

"Yeah, sure," said Ike, feeling he'd pushed his obnoxiousness a bit too far and needed to retreat a little. After all, he didn't want everybody on his case.

"I got just one question," said Bo. "How we gonna split up and still do all this stuff? We only got the one van."

"You and Fletch can take it," Alice said. "Me and Ike can walk to the police station. Look in the phone book, find a quick-print place—you can drop Fletch off—and then you can see about finding a sporting-goods store."

Bo looked anxious. "How am I supposed to find my way around this city? I mean, I don't know where anything is."

"Ask directions."

"I *hate* asking directions!"

Alice sighed. "All right, look. *You* get the flyers and Fletch'll go looking for a sporting-goods store. How's that? That all right, Fletch?"

"That's fine," said Fletch. "That's perfect."

"And we'll all meet back at the Holiday Inn around— six-thirty?"

"You want to synchronize our watches?" said Ike. But as soon as he had, he was sorry. Why, for crying out loud, did he always—always!—have to be a royal pain in the butt? Have to sneer and be such a wise guy? Sometimes—you know?—he even ticked himself off.

Alice stood up from the table. "You ready?"

"Ready," said Ike.

"I'll get the check," Fletch offered.

"Don't skimp on the tip," said Bo. He'd half-turned in his seat and was staring again—intrigued, infatuated—at the waitress. When she smiled, Bo grinned. "I bet she's not *really* from Albany," he said.

10

"Do what you want," said Alice.

"It's just that I—"

"Do what you *want!*"

They'd found their way, no problem, to Capitol Square, and got the final directions to police headquarters from a dapper old man with a gray walrus mustache and an ebony walking stick. But then, as they were about to step inside and see about filing a Missing Person report, Ike suddenly announced that he'd wait outside. Alice could go in by herself. He had a thing about police stations, he told her. He didn't like them. Not since the first time he'd been arrested. They gave him the creeps.

"So I'll meet you right here," said Ike.

With a curt, irritated nod, Alice left him standing on the steps and vanished through the front door.

Ike looked around for somewhere to sit down but couldn't find a bench, so he decided to take a short walk, make a loop around the square, and come right back.

Since it was late on a Saturday afternoon, there wasn't much activity now in this part of Richmond. During the week, Ike imagined, there were probably crowds clogging the sidewalks, buses coughing up fumes, and municipal and state cars nosing in and out of the city-owned garage-decks. Private cars prowling for parking spots. The Virginia State Capitol sat right across the street, at the top of a knoll. And over there was City Hall. Over there was the courthouse: the John Marshall Courts Building.

On his first hike around the area—it took him ten minutes—Ike passed only a handful of people.

Back at police headquarters again, he wondered how long

Alice was going to be gone. And felt a pang of guilt for having let her go inside alone.

Sometimes you really *are* a twit, he told himself.

He shrugged and began a second circuit of the square, but then changed his mind and walked up the knoll toward the Capitol building, found a green wooden bench, and sat down. He'd wait another ten minutes, then go back and see if Alice was finished.

As he sat there, feeling antsy and wishing he still smoked so that he'd have something to do, Ike heard a loud blast of radio music from a passing car. Quavery electric guitar, bluesy. Stevie Ray Vaughan maybe, or Eric Clapton. And then Ike was thinking about the first time he'd actually heard Del play her guitar. Back home, in the house on Farragut Street. . . .

She was sitting in the living room on a straight-backed chair, one leg crossed over the other, bottom lip bulged out, eyes screwed up in concentration. Ike watched her fingers wriggling nimbly on the frets, sliding up and down the neck, strumming chords and picking out silvery clear single notes, and he felt almost . . . dizzy. Man, she could really *do* it.

He asked her where she learned to play like that, and she answered, "From this old blues guy I met in Milwaukee. He was a neighbor, and I kept pestering him to show me some stuff."

Which sounded plausible enough . . . except that a week later, Ike overheard Bo Cudhy ask Del the same question and she told *him* that she'd learned everything she knew about playing guitar from a blind woman in Detroit.

The more Ike got to know Del (or rather, the longer that she lived with him and Alice, he never felt that he really *knew* her) the clearer it became that she was a phenomenal liar. Day by day her stories altered, her life history fluctuated, nothing ever synched. She kept inventing and reinventing herself the same way that she wrote her song lyrics:

drafting, scratching things out, scribbling things in—changing, always changing.

Because Alice liked Del and was charmed by her and so pleased to have a good girlfriend living in the house, she chose to ignore Del's fabrications. She never challenged her. Neither did Ike, but for another reason.

Though he'd never told (and would never tell) Alice this, he *admired* Del for being such a liar.

Actually, what he admired about her most was the way that she kept revising her identity. Concocting the biography she wanted—take it or leave it—and scrapping the one she'd been handed. Whatever it truly was.

Ike had to admit that Del's way of coping with her orphan's fate was far cooler than his own way, which was to act miserable, critical, sarcastic, cranky, and selfish. And it was probably a lot more satisfying, too. Del's way. Fun, even.

So he admired her. Enormously.

But meanwhile he treated Del like he treated everybody else: with chilly aloofness, keeping her at arm's distance. Because if you let down your guard for somebody, you'd finally have to let it down for everybody. At least that's how Ike saw things. You couldn't blow your cover. You just couldn't.

But now Del was missing, and it was possible—entirely possible!—that he might never see her again. And it was driving him nuts that he'd never told her just how much he admired her. Or how cool, in his opinion, she was.

Ike checked the time and realized he'd been on the bench already for twenty minutes. From where he was sitting, he couldn't see whether Alice had come out of police headquarters. Better get back over there and find out.

But as he was hurrying down the steep walk, he caught a glimpse of someone just up ahead, crossing the empty street, and his eyes bugged out.

It was her!

It was Del!

Cupping his hands around his mouth, he bellowed her name, then began sprinting.

"Del! Wait! *Del!*"

She didn't stop, though, or turn around.

Ike leaped down the brick steps at the end of the walk, hit the sidewalk with a teeth-clicking jolt, then took off again, running at his top speed. He darted into the street. Then, with a horn's blast and the squeal of metal and rubber, a minivan braked sharply. Less than a foot away from Ike. The driver stared at him, her expression translating rapidly from horror to wrath. He raised a shaky, apologetic hand and ran off again.

As he reached the curb, Ike's heart was pounding and his mouth was dry, but at least Del was standing there, looking at him quizzically, like she'd never laid eyes on him before.

Which she hadn't.

Because it wasn't Del Schofield. Just a red-haired, slightly-built young woman dressed in a lime windbreaker and black jeans. "What's your *problem*?" she asked.

"I thought you were somebody else," said Ike. "Sorry."

She gave him a dismissive glance, shook her head, and walked away.

With a long, disappointed sigh, Ike turned to head back up the street, but was startled to find his sister, Alice, right there behind him, standing with her head cocked to the side and a hand on her hip.

"You almost got killed," she said. "And I nearly had a heart attack."

"You seen that, huh?"

Alice glanced past Ike's shoulder, at the girl he'd chased. "From the back she *does* look like Del. Kind of." Alice smiled slowly. "But her hair's not red enough."

"Yeah, well." Ike assumed his practiced scowl. "So. Are you done? What happened?"

"They took down all the information, but . . . you know. Del's not a resident, she could be anywhere. Blah-blah-blah. But they phoned the hospitals for me. And the city jail. I

51

thought that was pretty decent of them. So at least we know she's not in either place. That's something."

Ike nodded. "Motel now?"

"Yeah, let's. Then we'll call out for pizza."

They didn't speak again during the walk back to the Holiday Inn, but Ike got the impression that Alice liked him suddenly a good deal more than she had in quite a while.

Probably because she'd seen him running like a crazy person after someone he'd mistaken for Del Schofield, and for nearly being run over in the process.

But he wished she hadn't seen that.

Showing his sister that he cared was embarrassing. It was really, really embarrassing.

Really.

11

According to the pink neon clock in a café window, it was a few minutes before eight o'clock. The sky, raveled with fishbellied clouds, had begun growing dark.

"What do you think?" Alice asked. "Are we just wasting our time?"

"No," said Fletch. "We're not. Think positive."

"I guess."

From her shoulder bag she withdrew another quick-print flyer (HAVE YOU SEEN THIS GIRL?) and passed it to Fletch, who deftly taped it on all sides to the curved surface of a lamppost. When he looked at Alice again, she was gazing off into space with a deep-furrowed frown.

"What's the matter, kiddo?"

"Nothing."

"Come on."

"Nothing is the matter—all right?"

"All right," said Fletch.

But just as they moved on again, ambling further down the sidewalk toward the next streetlight, Alice suddenly blurted, "We're not going to find her! This was a dumb, stupid, ridiculous idea! We don't know *what* we're doing!"

Fletch said, "Yeah, we do. We're taping up flyers on our way back to the club. And when we get there, we hook up with Bo and your crazy brother—then we hand out some more paper and talk to people. Sounds like a plan to me. And with any luck—"

"But what if we don't *have* any?"

"Like I said, kiddo, think positive."

"What's with this 'kiddo' stuff?" Despite her mood, Alice laughed. "Since when did you start calling me 'kiddo'?"

Fletch seemed to blush (in the ashy, fading light, it was impossible for Alice to be absolutely certain, but he *seemed* to), then, abruptly, he tore off another length of packing tape. "Flyer," he said, not meeting her eyes.

Alice reached into her bag and pulled yet another one out.

Several blocks away:

"How ya doin'?" said Bo to a passing couple, dreamy-looking hand-holders, both of them wearing college T-shirts. Hers from William and Mary, his from the University of Richmond. "Can I give you folks one of these? Don't worry, I'm not sellin' nothin'." Smiling, Bo thrust a flyer at the young woman, who accepted it, but with deep suspicion. "That's a friend of ours," he added, his finger pointing at Del's murky picture. "We sorta lost her a couple weeks ago in your fair city. Seen her around?"

They sure hadn't.

"Well, would you hold on to that flyer? Thanks! And if you *do* see her—that's her name, right there: Del—if you do see our friend Del, would you give us a call? That's the number, it's local, so you don't have to spend, like, any money. Hey, thanks!"

They were half a block away already, and Bo was calling after them.

"Thanks! Thanks a lot!"

Meanwhile, across the street, Ike Fuelle passed one of his flyers to a fat, completely bald man who'd just got out of his white Cadillac. Ike didn't say a word. Just handed him the flyer, scowled, and walked on. Without glancing at it, the fat man wadded it up, then tossed it into a trash can.

"This is a big waste," Ike groused at the next corner when Bo had crossed the street and joined him.

"Give it some time, my man. We just got started."

Then: " 'Scuse me," Bo said, striding past Ike to accost a trio of white-haired women who were coming down the steps from an Italian restaurant, negotiating their way slowly on account of their age and high heels. They were all dressed up for 1959, in Harriet Nelson dresses, and exuded sweet perfume. " 'Scuse me, but can I give you one of these? Ladies, don't worry, I'm not sellin' anything. That's a friend of ours. We sorta lost her . . ."

Ike shook his head and walked on.

When he and Bo arrived finally at the Moon Lamp, they spotted Alice handing out flyers to high-school kids and college students in the ragged, clumped-up line that had formed outside. Already some of the flyers were lying crumpled on the pavement or flipping around at ankle level in a small breeze. Bo snatched up those discards, carefully smoothed them out on his thigh, and stuck them away with his own cache in a manila envelope. "These suckers aren't cheap," he told Ike. Who sneered.

"Hey, troops." It was Fletch, suddenly there on the corner with them. "I just talked to the guy working the door. Mouse put us all on the comp list, so we can go on inside any time we want."

"Hope the band is decent," said Bo.

"Yeah, well—don't pay too much attention to them, all right? What we're trying to find is somebody that maybe seen us play here with Del, then maybe seen her again later on somewhere."

Bo looked as if he'd been unjustly accused of a major felony. "Hey! I know what we're trying to do. You don't have to tell me."

Behind them the club doors opened, and the crowd, glad-buzzing, began moving forward.

Ike, Fletch, and Bo stood back and watched, Bo wincing every time another flyer was balled up and tossed away.

Alice walked along with the line, quick-stepping now and speaking to a small, pink-haired girl in an extra-large red T-shirt and faded jeans with both knees torn out. When the girl passed through the door and into the club, Alice beckoned to Ike, Bo, and Fletch.

"That girl?" she said when they came over. "Seen Del!"

"Where?" all three asked.

"On the island."

"What island?" said Fletch.

"Where you played. Sunday afternoon?"

Fletch said, "Yeah? So?"

"She seen Del *taking a walk with somebody!* Remember you said that you couldn't find her? Well, that girl seen Del walking around the island with a guy who sounds exactly like our Mister Jude the Orphan Boy. Dressed all in black, with an aspirin face."

They stood around thinking about that, till finally, "He kidnapped her, didn't he?" said Bo. "That's what we're all afraid of, isn't it? Even though we don't say it. Well, I'm saying it. That creep kidnapped her!"

"We don't know that," Alice said, her expression suddenly anxious again. "For all we know, Del could be . . . crazy in love with him. The guy could be the greatest guy on earth. So great that she forgot all about us."

"Let's hope that's it," said Fletch.

"Yeah," said Bo. "Let's."

Ike Fuelle, eyes blazing like he wanted to strangle somebody, *anybody*, turned and strode across the sidewalk and into the Moon Lamp.

They passed the next four hours wandering the dance floor, hanging around the juice bar and the video-game room, and stopping briefly at crowded, pushed-together tables on the balcony. Showing their flyers, asking about Del.

Quite a few people they talked to remembered seeing her two weeks earlier, either when she'd performed at the club or at the free Sunday concert on Brown's Island, and nearly all of them gave her unsolicited rave reviews. But nobody remembered seeing her again.

Several times during the evening, Mouse Mineo put the flyer on the closed-circuit TV monitors, and twice between band sets, Alice nervously went on stage and made a brief announcement, a plea for information.

"All for nothing!" she said now, pressing the palm of a hand against her forehead. It was twenty past midnight, and she'd rendezvoused with Fletch and her brother in Mouse's little cork-walled office.

"I'm surprised at you, Alice," said Fletch. "I am. Really. I didn't think you'd give up so quick."

"Who says I'm giving up? I'm just . . . discouraged."

"We only got here today! Jeez. Let's see what happens tomorrow. With all those flyers around, we're bound to get some calls."

Alice nodded, but without enthusiasm.

Ike, sitting by himself in a corner, nursed his flat Coke and stared down morosely.

The walls shook with the muffled crash of live music. When the office door opened suddenly and Mouse appeared, the sound thundered in behind him with almost physical force. "Any luck?" he asked, fiddling with his rings.

"Not so far," said Alice.

But Fletch said, "Somebody'll remember something."

"How long do you guys plan on staying?"

"Through Sunday, I guess," said Fletch.

"Well, come on back tomorrow night if you want to. Be some different people. Maybe your luck'll change."

He gave a shrug and left.

"Luck," said Alice, disgusted.

"Let's get some sleep," Fletch said. "We're all flat-out exhausted. Where's Bo?"

"Probably out front listening to the stupid band," said Ike.

It was the first thing he'd said in half an hour.

He felt even more depressed than Alice looked.

"Well, let's go collect him, and get the heck outta here," said Fletch.

But when they scanned the dance floor, they couldn't find Bo. And he wasn't at the juice bar, or in the video-game room, or up on the balcony. They looked everywhere twice and finally went outside, peering up and down the street.

No Bo.

"Wonderful," said Ike. "Just great. Now *he's* missing?"

They were standing on the corner shivering—the temperature had dropped to forty degrees and they were wearing T-shirts—when Fletch slowly smiled, crookedly, and said, "Follow me."

They crossed the street and went inside the corner luncheonette where they'd had their strategy session. And found Bo seated in a back booth with the long tall waitress—from Albany—with the flyaway black hair.

Bo flicked a hand in greeting when he saw his friends, wholly ignoring their peeved expressions. "Guys? I want you to meet Ramona Pruitt. She says you can call her Mona, but I think *Ra*-mona is way cooler. Since I never met one before. Ramona? That's Alice, that's Fletch, and Mister Sunshine over there, that's Ike."

Ramona smiled and nodded.

"We've been looking all over for you," said Alice.

"Yeah, yeah," said Bo, "I figured as much. But don't y'all give me no grief till y'all hear what I got to say." His smile kept inching higher. "All right? Now listen up, y'all."

Ike leaned forward, putting his face close to Bo's. "You say that one more time, just once, and I'm gonna pop you in the mouth."

"Okay. All right." Placing a hand on Ike's shoulder, Bo lightly pushed. Ike stepped back from the table. Then, "Ramona, here," said Bo, "hasn't only *seen* this guy Jude we're looking for, she knows how to *find* him!"

Impulsively, Fletch flung an arm around Alice and hugged her. "And you didn't believe in luck! Shame on you, kiddo!"

12

Ever since Bo Cudhy had first seen long tall Ramona Pruitt—seen her girl-next-door pretty face and heard her musical southernisms—he'd been trying to think of a casual way to see her again. That evening, wandering around the Moon Lamp doing his detective routine, Bo was sorely tempted just to slip away to her luncheonette. But then he suddenly remembered what time it was and figured that she wouldn't still be working, that her shift would have ended hours ago.

Finally, though, after he grew sick of asking people the same question ("Seen Del?") and getting the same negative responses, and especially once he decided that he couldn't—absolutely could not—stand to listen to Mouse Mineo's wretched house band for even one second longer, Bo gave himself permission to take a break. He weaved through the club crowd and ducked furtively out the side door. That was at about a quarter of twelve.

On his way across the street, he decided that he'd simply ask the cashier when the tall waitress would be working again. Then somehow he would make it his business to drop by. Unless, of course, she didn't work any shifts over the weekend. But he didn't want to think about that.

Because he was so convinced that the waitress—*his* waitress—wouldn't still be there, Bo didn't even look around for her when he came in. She *was* still there—topping somebody's coffee at a square table set flush against the brick wall—but he didn't notice her. He walked straight to the cashier's station. There was a shallow bowl of green and blue mints on the counter, and several yellowing *Far Side* cartoons taped to the register.

The cashier was an unhappy- (or perhaps just tired-) looking man, about forty, with very fine yellow hair and cheeks waffled with acne scars. Silkscreened on his black T-shirt was a big picture of Moe Howard's head, the guy from the *Three Stooges*. "There was a waitress here this afternoon," said Bo. "Very tall—" he reached a hand over his head, even though she wasn't *that* tall—"and she has black hair."

"Ramona," said the cashier.

"Ramona?" repeated Bo, instantly delighted.

The cashier stood up, then stood on his toes, and called, "Ramona!"

Bo was amazed—she was actually still there?

It turned out that Ramona Pruitt had been scheduled to get off work at eight, but when another waitress phoned in sick, she'd agreed to stay till midnight.

Talk about good luck.

And it kept getting better. . . .

"When Bo came in looking for me," Ramona was saying now, "I thought perhaps he'd left something behind when y'all were here this afternoon. Or I guess it's yesterday afternoon already."

"Perhaps," said Bo, pointing to Ramona and smiling at Fletch, Alice, and Ike, in turn. "You hear that? She says *perhaps*. Like we'd say *maybe*—right? '*Maybe* he left something behind.' But she says *perhaps*. Who says *perhaps*? I *love* how she talks!"

"Shut up," said Ike.

"Go on," Alice urged Ramona. "Please."

"But then Bo said he needed to ask me something. But he wouldn't say what—not till I clocked out. He said he'd wait." She turned to Bo, seated across the table and pressed tight against the wall (Ike and Fletch had squeezed onto the bench beside him). Then she grinned at him. Bo wasn't sure whether it was with amusement or affection, but it didn't really matter which. He'd take either one.

"I figured I'd show her the flyer," said Bo. And right away

he noticed Alice Fuelle—on the opposite side of the table, next to Ramona—move her mouth into a small, ironic smile. Yeah, Alice saw clear through *that* smokescreen, all right. Oh well.

"And as soon as I saw the picture on the flyer," Ramona said, "I remembered Bo! It's funny, but I *thought* he looked familiar. You, too," she added, nodding at Fletch now.

"Ramona seen us play at the club with Del! She was *there* that night!" Bo said. "And so naturally I asked her about this Orphan Jude, thinking maybe she seen Del talking to him there."

Ramona said, "But I hadn't."

"Then I *described* the creep—"

"And it sounded exactly like a guy that I met just about a month ago. His name," Ramona said, "is Jude Hayser."

"Where do we find him?" asked Ike. He'd already started to get up from the bench.

"Wait a second," said Alice. She turned back to Ramona. "How'd you meet him? Did he come in here?"

"Later on he did. But I first met him out by where he lives, in an old house on the James River. Somewhere out on Route Five, north of town."

"How far?" asked Fletch.

"Twenty minutes. But look, people," said Ramona, "I don't think I could *find* it in the dark. I want to help you, but it's got to be tomorrow. In daylight I'm pretty sure I'd know the place when I saw it. But in the dark—don't bet on it. There are dozens of little side roads, dirt roads, all of them winding off to farms and old plantations."

"So you met him at his *house*?" said Alice.

"Yeah, but not exactly. See, I should tell you, I guess—I go to college. I'm not a full-time waitress, I'm a film major. And a friend of mine asked me to help her make a video for some local band."

"You didn't tell me that!" said Bo. "Cool! Maybe you could make one for Del." Then he frowned. "After we find her, of course."

"I wasn't in *charge* or anything," Ramona continued. "Basically I was just a gofer, but it was fun. There were six of us in the crew, and the four guys in the band. And we just drove out Route Five looking for a big field. *Any* big, open field would do. So the musicians could all run around, and flap their arms, and make believe they were playing guitar in the great outdoors. You know the drill."

Ike leaned forward, planting his elbows on the table. "But how did you meet—"

"I'm *getting* there," said Ramona, looking him square in the eye. "All *right?*"

Ike lifted his hands, palms out, in a gesture of surrender. Then he sat back. "All right."

Bo couldn't tear his eyes away from Ramona Pruitt's face. It was so pretty, so animated! And dig her eyes. Large and slightly bulging, a dark green color, the whites amazingly white.

He realized (and it hit him like a bolt, a startling insight) that he was looking at Ramona the way that Ike used to look at Del Schofield. And he thought, Whoa—*now* I get it!

Forcing his gaze away from Ramona, Bo glanced sideways. And noticed that Ike had picked up the glass salt and pepper shakers and was nervously clicking them both together.

Bo thought, Poor Ike, man. What a phony!

13

"... three cars," Ramona was saying. "Well, two cars and a big old Dodge van. My friend Lisa was driving that, and I was riding with her. We were leading the way, even though, like I said, none of us knew where we were going. What we were looking for was a place that didn't have 'Private Property, No Trespassing' signs nailed on every tree. So we drove along for a while ..."

... till Lisa spotted a narrow dirt road up ahead, just off to the right. She pulled over and stopped, and the two cars in the caravan parked behind them. Everybody climbed out and took a look around. There were no posted signs, not even a mailbox. So far, so good. But what they really wanted was an open field, and the view toward the river was blocked by snarly hedgerows. So before they got their hopes too high, Ramona, Lisa, and two crewies took a short hike up the dirt cutoff....

"It snaked around for a couple of hundred yards," said Ramona, "and these old, wild bushes and weed trees crowded in from both sides—but we finally came around this one bend and there it was, exactly what we wanted. This absolutely enormous, unplanted field. It must have been, I don't know, twenty acres. Tall grass and a gajillion wildflowers stretching clear to the James. And in the middle distance, we could see an old, dilapidated farmhouse. But ..."

... there was no sign of habitation. Even so, Ramona suggested to the others that they go check it out. What if there *was* somebody actually living there, some old crackpot who'd come charging out with a shotgun the minute he spotted trespassers on his sacred property? But Lisa said no, forget it, the place was *obviously* abandoned. Just look at it! Who would *live there*? There weren't even phone wires. Lisa prevailed, and the house was declared empty.

Hiking back down the dirt track, they informed the others that they'd discovered a perfect spot for the video shoot. Within minutes, they parked the van and two cars at the edge of the hidden grassy acreage, and everybody started to unload equipment. The four scrawny band guys lugged out their guitars and set up a drum kit almost dead center in the field. Immediately, the drummer commenced walloping his tom-tom and crashing the cymbals. The two guitarists took off their shirts and greased their chests with baby oil. The bass player put on sunglasses, then fluffed his black Beethoven hair. *They* were ready!

While the tapes were being loaded into the camcorders, Lisa told her crew to just shoot randomly at first. Zoom in on faces and stock poses. Improvise. Ramona was put in charge of the boom-box, which meant all she had to do was load the disc tray and blast the band's self-issued CD single; she programmed it to repeat, and that was that. . . .

"So was the band any good?" Bo asked.

"Tell you the truth," said Ramona, "I don't really remember. I guess I tuned it out. I'm not really into music."

"Jude," said Ike, leaning over the table on his folded arms. The salt and pepper shakers were encircled. "I thought you were going to tell us about *Jude*."

"And now," Ramona said, a bit sharply, "I'm actually going to do that."

First, though, she took a little sip from her iced tea. Then, "I went back to the van to get something, another tape, I think." Ramona continued, "And when I turned around from the hatch, this guy was standing right behind me. Twenty years old, maybe. Dressed entirely in black. Very skinny. And very pale."

"Like a vampire, right?" said Fletch.

"Right. And he scared me half to death, standing right there behind me. . . ."

Ramona noticed, while her heart decelerated, that the stranger was looking intently at her chest. That really annoyed her, and she extended her right arm in front of her, moving her hand back and forth like a windshield wiper. "Hel-lo," she said, giving the word a mocking edge. Like, Hel-lo in there, wake up!

He smiled.

"Are we trespassing?" she asked him.

"Uh-huh," said the stranger, but Ramona couldn't tell if he was irked or hostile or couldn't have cared less.

"We're film students from Richmond," Ramona said. "We didn't think anybody was around."

"That's all right," he said, and the way that he shrugged then was so casual and sincere that Ramona finally relaxed. She introduced herself.

"Jude Hayser," he said, and they shook hands. By that time, Lisa and the guys in the crew had noticed Jude Hayser's arrival and were on their way over to see what was going on. . . .

"Tell them about the grave," said Bo.

"What grave?" said Fletch. *"Grave?"*

"Let her talk," said Ike, and Ramona favored him with a small smile.

Instantly, Bo was jealous.

"Jude said it was okay to use the field," Ramona began again, "and he even hung out there with us for awhile. Well, mostly he hung out with me. Jude never left my side. Then about an hour after he showed up, another man arrived . . .

. . . in a pearl-gray Audi, pulling in and parking behind Lisa's van. He was speaking on a cellular phone and didn't immediately get out of his car. Ramona glanced at him, but couldn't really see too much; sunlight rubbed the windshield.

Jude Hayser looked annoyed; Ramona heard him curse softly under his breath. Then he strode over to the Audi. At last, the driver got out. He was a roly-poly man in a white dress shirt, a red speckled necktie, and dark blue suit pants. His brown hair was thinning on top, and his hairline had receded dramatically. Ramona guessed that he was thirty-five or forty, somewhere around there. He smiled and put out his hand, but Jude didn't take it.

"What's going on out here, Jude?" asked the newcomer. "You shootin' a movie?"

"Not me," said Jude. "What is it today, Mr. Odet? I wish you wouldn't keep showing up. I don't mean to be un-friendly, but I already told you what I told you. And noth-ing's changed. Or is apt to gonna."

Odet gave Jude Hayser a withering look—Ramona saw it, and she instantly disliked the man. She would have bet money that he was either a lawyer or a real estate agent. . . .

"He was a realtor," Ramona said now. "He even gave me his card. Of course."

"Do you still have it?" said Alice.

"It's probably at my aunt's house. That's where I live. With my Aunt Ardeth. I could look for it—his card. But he'd be in the phone book: Greg Odet."

"Is this important?" said Ike. "I'm still waiting for the part about a grave."

They'd all been sitting in the back booth for half an hour, and it was almost one in the morning. Already the cashier had swung around twice, saying they'd have to leave shortly. It was closing time.

Now, most of the lights suddenly cut off. The place was dark except for a single, high-wattage bulb dangling behind the counter.

"Can we go someplace and finish talking?" Alice asked Ramona.

"You could follow me back to my aunt's house, if you want. We could hang out there."

"All right," said Fletch, "but what kind of car do you drive? We need a lift to the Holiday Inn to pick up our van."

"It'll be a tight squeeze," said Ramona, "but I think we can all fit."

She had a Mitsubishi Mirage, and it was a *very* tight squeeze, but mercifully only a short ride to the motel. There, everybody got out except Bo. He stayed with Ramona, sitting with her up front.

"So," he said, once the others were behind them in Alice's van and both vehicles were rolling west through the dark streets of Richmond. "You ever get up to New Jersey?"

"Never."

They passed a city park, then an enormous theater with minarets on the roof, a university library, a Seven-Eleven, then a mile of commercial buildings interspersed with neighborhood restaurants, most of those dark by now. There wasn't much traffic or many people out on the street.

Bo sat quietly for a long while, racking his brain for just the right thing to say. Finally, when nothing too brilliant came to mind, he said, "What did you mean, you don't like music? You don't like *any* kind of music, at *all*?"

Ramona laughed.

Man, he loved it when she did that! But he told himself to watch out; he didn't want her thinking that he was "cute."

That would be the kiss of death.

So to counteract the cuteness, he pulled on his knuckles, like a movie gangster, till his joints popped.

14

In the kitchen of the split-level house where Ramona Pruitt lived with her aunt, they were all grouped around a table with a wood-grain laminated top. Everything, from the bright pink refrigerator and the matching electric stove to the knotty pine cabinets, Waring blender, Mixmaster, frilly curtains, and pink, black, and white spatter-pattern linoleum floor, was 1950s deluxe. The walls were covered in aqua-colored Sanitas. And there was a sunburst clock.

As soon as they came in, Ramona put out a couple of large plastic bottles of Coke, glasses with ice, and a box of bakery cookies.

"You were telling us," said Alice, "about that real-estate guy."

"Sleazy Greg Odet," Ramona said. "Okay. Well . . ."

. . . He kept browbeating Jude, and Ramona couldn't believe how much, and how quickly, she despised the man. For one thing, he talked about Jude Hayser's private business right in front of her, which Ramona thought was unprofessional and crude. And for another thing, when he talked he sprayed the air with fine spittle—which she thought was gross. "Jude doesn't use this land," Odet said to Ramona, "it's just sitting here. Wasted. I could get him a million dollars for it. I bet you could find some use for a million dollars. Couldn't you, darlin'?"

Ramona didn't reply; it was a stupid question, and this was none of her business.

Jude Hayser finally told Odet that he was busy with his guests—meaning Ramona and the film crew and band—and that he couldn't spare him any more time.

That's when Odet turned nasty. "Fine, Mr. Hayser," he said. "I'll go. But let me leave you with a little warning. If you don't sell a.s.a.p., you're going to lose this property for back taxes. And you'll be out on your butt, mister, and no million dollars." He got back into his Audi, backed the car around, and left with a stone-spitting trail of dust.

Jude Hayser watched him go—stood there with his fists planted on his hips, making sure that Odet didn't change his mind suddenly and back up.

When he turned again to Ramona, his entire demeanor was different. Hayser was cool and sullen now, almost hostile. "How much longer are you people going to be?" he wanted to know.

"I'll go and check if you want," Ramona offered.

"It doesn't matter. Just leave soon as you're done, and please don't come back here again. Next time you *will* be trespassing."

He turned and walked up the road to his house, looking like a loose-jointed scarecrow come to life.

Later that afternoon, when the crew and the band were packing away equipment, Ramona fished out a boxed lunch she'd brought along but hadn't opened. "Be right back," she told Lisa.

Nobody answered when she knocked at Hayser's front door. She called his name repeatedly, then went around the side of the house to the backyard, where at last she found him. He was sitting on a small wrought-iron bench, hunched forward, elbows on his knees, staring at a fairly fresh grave. Nearby were a few low, round-topped limestone gravestones. A family plot.

When he realized that Ramona was behind him, Jude Hayser quickly stood up. She was afraid he'd be angry, but no, he smiled. "Were you looking for me? I'm sorry."

"I wanted to give you this," Ramona said, offering him the lunch, "as a little token of our appreciation. Ham sandwich, potato salad, and a brownie."

As Jude graciously accepted it, Ramona glanced past him, at the mounded grave. He saw her and looked there himself.

"My father," he said. "He died in June. Now they're both gone."

"Your mother? . . ."

"That grave just yonder. She passed on—it'll be two years next March."

"I'm sorry," said Ramona. "I know how you must feel. I lost both my parents, too."

That interested Jude Hayser. Very much. So much that Ramona felt suddenly nervous. He wanted to know when Ramona's parents had died, how old she'd been. Did she have any brothers or sisters. Hayser was more than just eager—he seemed . . . prying. It gave her the creeps.

And then he asked Ramona if she'd ever heard of Thomas Dunbar Lawrence and the Orphans' Migration. . . .

"Who?" said Ike. "The *what*?"

"The Orphans' Migration," said Ramona. "I told Jude I didn't know what on earth he was talking about, and right away he starts to tell me about something that happened sixty years ago."

"What?" said Alice.

"Some orphans' convention, or something. I didn't get much of it. 'Cause Lisa started beeping for me. So I thanked him again and said I had to get going, and he walked me back around to the road. . . ."

"And then he hit on her for a date," said Bo, making it sound like a capital offense.

"But I said I was already seeing somebody," said Ramona.

"Even though she really wasn't." Bo nodded several times. "She just didn't want to go out with him."

"That's the truth," Ramona agreed. "Even though it wasn't that I didn't *like* him. He just . . . wasn't my type."

"And there was something creepy about him," said Bo.

"There was," Ramona said. She pressed her lips together, clenched her jaw. "Definitely."

Alice said, "But so how'd he find you again?"

"Earlier, when he was watching us make the video? I told him I lived in Richmond. And where I worked."

"How many times did he drop around there to see you?"

"Just twice. The first time I sat with him for a couple of minutes, and he tried to show me these old newspaper clippings he'd brought along. But I was workin'! I couldn't just sit down with a customer and look at some old papers. He got pretty annoyed and left. And the second time—"

"Listen to this," said Bo. "The second time was the same night we played at the Moon Lamp."

Ramona said, "It was. Jude came in around eight o'clock. Took a table. But when I went over for his order, he pretended he didn't recognize me. When I brought him his sandwich, though, he was all friendly again. Wanted to know how long I'd be working. I said for a while still, and then he asked me could he wait around. I said I wished he wouldn't, and then—then I told him that I was going to the Moon Lamp once I got off. Which was the truth, but I made it sound like I was meeting my boyfriend there. Which wasn't the truth. Anyhow, Jude left as soon as he'd finished eating. Gave me a nice tip, and I haven't seen him since."

"Not even at the Moon Lamp?" said Ike. "Later on?"

"I didn't see him there, no. But that doesn't mean he *wasn't* there."

"What I figure," said Bo, "is that he went to the club intending to meet Ramona, maybe check out her boyfriend . . . but then he ended up talking to Del instead."

Fletch thought about that for a moment, then said, "Yeah. It's possible."

Alice—who, by this time, looked drop-dead tired—rose from the table. "Well, I guess we can't do anything else for now." She looked at Ramona. "What's a good time to come by and pick you up?"

"You don't have to come all the way over here again. I'll meet you at your motel. Say, eleven? Is that too early?"

"That's perfect," said Ike. "Then we'll go have a look at

this Jude Hayser." He stood up too, followed by Fletch, and finally, reluctantly, Bo.

As they were all thanking Ramona, and while she was asking them whether they needed directions back to the Holiday Inn, a woman padded down the carpeted passageway outside the kitchen. She was tall, wiry, and small-faced, with short-cropped brown hair and a pointed nose; she looked to be somewhere in her late forties. She was wearing a shiny bathrobe with a dark Chinese print and pink bedroom slippers, and she seemed startled to find so many strangers.

"Aunt Ardeth," said Ramona, "I want you to meet some people from New Jersey." She said everybody's name, then added, "And this is my aunt Ardeth."

"New Jersey," Ramona's aunt said. "I had kin lived up there for awhile. Let me remember. Is there a place called Elizabeth? That's where they lived. Cousins of mine, on my granddaddy Early's side of the family. Nice to meet you all!" She moved from the doorway into the kitchen. "Oh, Mona," she said, "you could've offered your friends something besides cookies! Would anybody like me to make some pancakes? It's no trouble!"

"We were just getting ready to leave," said Alice. "But thank you very much for the offer."

Then Aunt Ardeth said, "Did I hear somebody just mention the name Hayser a minute ago? I had a second cousin, one of the Pitt girls, the Raleigh-Durham Pitts, married someone named Hayser, I believe. Raymond Hayser. Of the Greensboro Haysers."

Ramona rolled her eyes. "We were talking about somebody named *Jude* Hayser," she said. "Lives out on Route Five, heading east toward Williamsburg."

"Oh, *Jude* Hayser!" said Aunt Ardeth. "The boy on TV."

Dead silence. Till finally, "If you all just want to sit yourselves down again," said Ramona, "I'll get out the pancake mix."

15

Ever since his parents died, at least twice a month—while he was sleeping—Ike Fuelle would burst spontaneously into flames. It always happened the same way. He'd be in the middle of a dream and begin to feel . . . afraid. Moments later, terror would course through him like snake venom, he'd begin sweating abnormally, then—whoosh!—he'd go up like a torch, screaming as the orange fire raced across his flesh, cooking him. He knew that he ought to drop to the ground and roll madly to smother the flames, but he couldn't move!

And as soon as he realized that, he would know that he was still dreaming.

At five past six that Saturday morning, Ike erupted in flames again and woke with a convulsive groan. His T-shirt was drenched, his hair was damp, and his scalp felt itchy. When he touched a hand to his forehead, the perspiration there was hot.

The bedsheet was twisted crazily around his feet and calves. Ike kicked viciously several times and shook it loose. Then he rolled out of bed and crossed to the bathroom. He drank several glasses of water.

At last the dream of being on fire began to recede. Ike frowned into the sink mirror. He thought, Wait a second, and went back out. Bo was sleeping quietly in one of the double beds, but Fletch wasn't. Ike glanced toward the connecting door to Alice's room, shook his head, and returned to the bathroom.

He brushed his teeth, shaved, then took a shower, an ice-cold one.

Afterward, he sat in the room with a bath towel wrapped

around his middle, watching early-morning cartoons with the volume muted. Bo started to make chewing sounds in his sleep. Ike felt like pegging a Gideons' Bible at him, but instead he got dressed and rode the elevator down to the lobby. The coffee shop was open, so Ike took a table and paged through a complimentary copy of *USA Today*. Every few minutes he'd look at his watch. 7:12. Quarter after. Twenty after. 7:23.

It was a long time—hours to go!—till eleven o'clock. Then Ramona would come and they all would finally go meet this Jude Hayser.

No matter how hard Ike tried to concentrate on some story in the newspaper, his attention kept slipping. He'd think of Del, about the time he walked into the house and she was sitting around in just a white halter top and cut-offs. Or remember the soulful expression on her face the first time she'd sing a new song, lost completely in the lyrics.

The waiter came by with more coffee and refilled Ike's cup.

It was seven-thirty. Well, not quite. 7:28.

Ike read a celebrity column, his gaze skipping over the names in boldface type: Richard Gere. Madonna. Oliver Stone. Geena Davis.

Thomas Dunbar Lawrence.

Ike thought for a second that he'd actually seen that name, but no. He'd only imagined it.

Thomas Dunbar Lawrence, Ike thought now, remembering the not-entirely-coherent story that Aunt Ardeth told them a few hours ago. She'd been recapping a program she'd seen on *Unsolved Mysteries* months earlier.

Ike looked at his watch: 7:32.

"Mind if I sit?"

It was Fletch, already sliding onto the chair opposite. He had on the same clothes he'd been wearing when they got back to the motel, and his beard was stubbly—he looked bleary-eyed.

Coolly, Ike watched him pick up a breakfast menu.

"Alice and I were talking all night," Fletch said after he laid the menu back down. "I don't think I'm gonna bother trying to sleep now."

In a dead voice, Ike said, "Uh-huh."

"What's that supposed to mean?"

"Nothing."

"Your sister and I were just talking, *talking*. That's *all*."

"Hey. It's none of *my* business *what* you were doing in her room," said Ike.

"Coffee," Fletch growled to the waiter. "And lemme have a small orange juice."

"Yes, sir. Thank you, sir."

Fletch sat back and stared across the table at Ike, who gave an indifferent shrug, then found his place in the newspaper. He read about somebody getting a salary of six million dollars just to star in another dumb action movie.

When he looked at his watch again, it was 7:35.

16

Alice Fuelle generally woke up at ten minutes past eight. Her body clock was so reliable that she never needed an alarm. Usually she'd go to bed sometime between eleven-thirty and midnight, and have a full eight hours' rest. But even when she got to sleep much later—as she did this morning, dozing off around five A.M.—she'd still wake up at her regular time, eight-ten on the dot, refreshed and ready for another day.

When Alice opened her eyes and realized that she was still wearing yesterday's clothes, she remembered where she was and rolled over, glancing toward the other double bed. The spread was mussed, but Fletch was no longer sitting on it. Two soda cans stood on the lamp table, so did an empty bag of chips, and crumpled in the ashtray were several candy bar wrappers.

Fletch had got all that stuff from vending machines down the hall, just before he came knocking at Alice's door at 3:15 that morning, saying, "Kiddo? You still awake?"

Kiddo.

Smiling, Alice levered herself onto an elbow and called Fletch's name. No reply. So he wasn't in the bathroom. He was gone.

Now that she was certain she was alone, Alice flopped onto her back and smiled at the ceiling, idly counting the sprinkler nozzles. Then she closed her eyes.

Jeez, she wasn't imagining this, was she? No, Fletch was really interested—really! In *her*! And she had to admit that she found him attractive. Oh, yeah, very. She liked the way that he talked to her, the affectionate tone he'd started using, and she liked the gravelly sound of his voice, and she liked the way that he smiled.

It was all very weird, because she'd never thought about Fletch in a romantic way before. In fact, when he'd started coming over to the house in Jersey to play with Bo and Del, Alice hardly had paid any attention to him. She guessed now that it was because of his reputation. Here was a guy who'd been in a big-time rock-and-roll band, and he'd been tossed out for screwing up. For missing gigs, or for showing up drunk. Here was a guy who'd made a lot of money fast, then spent it all and had nothing to show for it.

No wonder Alice hadn't looked at him twice.

Somebody as altogether responsible as she was certainly would never fall in love with somebody as irresponsible as Fletch.

But now she had—she *had* fallen for him. So what did that mean?

Well, Alice didn't know exactly.

But, she told herself, people change. They do.

Fletch surely wasn't acting irresponsibly these past few days. So that meant he'd changed—didn't it? At least a little?

And maybe Alice herself had changed. Being around Del Schofield so much for a couple of months, that might have done it. Del may have been the catalyst. Alice, who'd never been spontaneous—who'd always considered options carefully, perhaps too carefully, and who'd methodically planned her days, her weeks, her *life*—had nevertheless found herself being secretly envious of Del's minute-to-minute impulsiveness last summer. Now, there was a girl who made things up as she went along, who *never* planned ahead. She did whatever she felt like doing whenever she felt like doing it. Even if it was foolish or dangerous.

Some of that Del quality might have—it must have!—rubbed off on Alice.

So be it, she thought.

Still smiling, she got out of bed, turned on the TV (wasn't that what you were *supposed* to do in a motel room in a strange city, first thing upon rising?), then went and took a long hot shower.

It was while she was standing under the hard spray, rinsing shampoo from her hair, that Alice's morning euphoria began to flicker. By the time she was toweling herself dry, she felt anxious again and sorely troubled. Not because of Fletch, or because of her tentative new feelings toward him; rather, because she'd been thinking about Del, and for a few minutes she'd almost—not quite, but almost—forgotten that Del was missing.

But now that inescapable fact, more potent because of its brief absence, came flooding back into Alice's brain. She stood very still in the billowing clouds of steam, then began to shiver.

A few minutes later, dressed in clean clothes and seated on the edge of her bed dragging a comb through her wet hair, Alice glanced at the empty soda cans on the lamp table. . . .

When Fletch appeared at her door, he apologized for bothering her so late—but he couldn't sleep, he said.

"Neither can I," Alice told him, then opened the door wider for him to step inside.

If he tried to kiss her then, she would have let him.

But he didn't. He just put down the cans and the junk food, sat on one of the beds, spread his hands, and asked Alice what she thought about Aunt Ardeth's story.

"Creepy."

"Agreed," Fletch said.

"You didn't see that program, did you?" she asked then.

"Unsolved Mysteries?" He shook his head. "I'd never even *heard* of it!"

"Robert Stack's the narrator," said Alice. "And every week there's, like, a few different weird stories—"

"Yeah, I gather. But I care about only one story in particular."

According to Aunt Ardeth's summary of the show (which

she'd only watched because it was "of local interest"), several dozen young men and women—perhaps as many as a hundred—had gathered on a farm near Richmond during the Great Depression. What had made the gathering noteworthy was this: each one of them was an orphan. Their leader was a mysterious man named Thomas Dunbar Lawrence, who'd rented the pasture from a farmer named Hobart Hayser. The orphans had pitched tents, built sanitation facilities, and patrolled the area to keep out nosy neighbors. But what were they all *doing* there, camped out on that farm? Nobody knew.

And then one morning, two weeks after the small tent city had been erected, somebody driving along Route 5 noticed smoke coming from the bull pasture. The tents were on fire! Dozens and dozens of tents, all of them in flames. Fire engines roared to the scene, but when the blaze had finally been extinguished, there wasn't a single corpse to be found. And no sign of the orphans anywhere. Where had they gone? Again, nobody knew. Or ever found out. They had simply vanished.

On that episode of *Unsolved Mysteries*, Hobart Hayser's great-grandson had been interviewed. The young man's name was Jude Hayser. He seemed a peculiar sort, Aunt Ardeth had thought, shy and angry at the same time. He'd also seemed very much enamored of the lore surrounding the lost orphans. Young Hayser had called the event the "Orphans' Migration," and had claimed—well, Aunt Ardeth couldn't remember exactly *what* he'd claimed, but it had something to do with traveling to another world, or another dimension, or something crazy like that. . . .

And Fletch, talking to Alice about it at four in the morning, said, "All I keep thinking about is that photograph you got from Dead Mary."

"Me, too," Alice said. "Me, too."

"Everybody who I showed the picture to this afternoon, all the guys at all those sporting-goods stores, every one of them told me the same thing: That nobody makes tents like that one anymore. That it had to be very old. Maybe fifty, sixty years."

Alice said, "That would make it—"

"The mid-nineteen-thirties. Depression days."

Fletch kept his eyes on hers, then wrinkled his forehead. . . .

Now, alone in her motel room at twenty minutes to nine, Alice was thinking once again about that photograph.

She put her comb down and went over to the writing desk, where she'd dumped her shoulder bag. She pulled out a bunch of flyers, put them aside, then dug her hand back in and took out her wallet.

Flipping through the celluloid windows, Alice drew out the snapshot of the large white canvas tent pitched in a gloomy attic.

Alice braced her elbows on the desk and studied the photograph. She looked at it, looked *into* it, staring hard, focusing intently, until her eyes began to feel strained.

Then, from behind her, she heard somebody shout, "Gasoline! It's time!" and she flinched. And when she turned around to look, Alice's head began to swim—bright, glittering threads and tiny explosions burst in front of her eyes.

Afraid that she'd fall, she reached to grab something for support, but missed. Somebody roughly snatched hold of her by an elbow. Yanked her upright.

"Hurry, now!" said a man's urgent voice. "It's time to burn the tents!"

17

Alice kept squeezing her eyes shut, then snapping them open, but nothing changed. Inexplicably, she was somewhere else—outdoors, in a vast open field. There was a bright half-moon, and the vast, black sky was spangled with an uncountable number of stars. The temperature was about fifty, with a chill breeze blowing. A breeze that carried the acrid, headache-making odor of gasoline.

I'm still dreaming, she thought. It's not eight-ten yet, and I'm still dreaming in my bed. Waking up was a dream. Showering was a dream. Looking at that photograph. Now this.

But it was unlike any dream Alice had ever had. Everything that happened around her—lank men in coveralls lugging heavy red gasoline cans, the contents sloshing; women in homespun, threadbare dresses all rushing forward together, holding hands, chattering—or sobbing—with excitement; mangy dogs running in circles, barking, confused by all the tumult—everything had a clarity, a *concreteness*, that she'd never experienced in any dream before.

She stumbled when a boy jostled against her. He was about sixteen, completely bald. Above his left eyebrow was a brown mole the size of a penny. His jeans were rolled up around his calves, and he was barefoot.

"You better not just stand there, girly," he said. "The Orphan Thomas wants us all to be in our tents in two minutes flat!" Then he ran off, squirting through the jam of bodies moving toward a double line of wall tents that faced each other across a broad strip of field grass.

Pitched like that, the tents reminded Alice of an army bivouac, or a carnival midway—though none of them were mottled with camouflage paint or decorated with freakish murals.

They were all plain white canvas tents.

Alice willed herself to follow the crowd and shortly found herself walking alongside a scrawny-necked man and a short, heavyset woman smoking a corncob pipe. Both were dressed in thin, worn-out clothing and had weathered, cracked faces.

They glanced at Alice, smiled nervously, then looked away. Because of their round-shouldered posture and their work-worn faces, she thought at first that they were in their late fifties. Now—although it was hard to be certain in the moonlight—she felt they probably weren't even twenty-five. Prematurely aged.

Women and men started to enter the tents in pairs. Some couples allowed dogs to come inside with them; others chased them, even kicked them, away. As each tent was occupied and its door flaps secured with tie-tapes, someone stationed beside it would hoist a big gasoline can and slop the canvas.

Finally, while Alice remained transfixed at one end of the grassy strip between the tents, the gasoline throwers paired off and entered tents of their own, which were then, in turn, liberally doused.

Alice realized that everyone was gone now. All the men and women had vanished inside tents, and the night air was oppressive with the smell of gasoline. The fumes stung her nostrils and throat when she breathed.

At the far end of the midway, a silhouetted man suddenly appeared from behind the last tent.

He was a tall, sticklike figure, and as Alice looked on with a spasm of fear, a flame bloomed from the man's left hand. Then it leaped to a thick wad of rags wrapped around the end of a broomstick.

The man started walking toward Alice, using his torch to set tents ablaze as he moved slowly forward.

The tents burst into fire with spectacular ferocity. Alice

couldn't understand how the man wasn't badly scorched. He never flinched, though—just kept right on walking, heading straight toward her. In the light from the fires, she could see his bony, grinning face; his crooked, gapped teeth; and his long, black hair blowing loosely behind him. He stopped when he spotted Alice, gazing at her in astonishment. "Why are you still out in this world, Sister?" he called above the roar of the flames.

She couldn't speak, not because this was a dream—it wasn't, Alice now knew for certain—but because she was terrified. By this man. And by those fires. The heat was intense, the red and yellow glare nearly blinding.

"I asked you, Sister," bellowed the man, "why are you still abiding here? We go now to a better world. Don't be frightened."

He extended his torch arm and yet another tent went up in a blaze, flame tongues licking through black, foamy smoke.

But suddenly, behind him, the fires all blended to create an arcing bridge across the midway and just above the man's head. Alarmed, he threw down his torch. Then he turned and raced back through the firestorm, which had ignited the field grass. With a roaring sound, the flames exploded toward Alice in a black-and-red gush of light and powerful heat.

She flung up her arms and screamed.

A moment later, she felt herself being *plucked* away.

When she opened her eyes again, she was back in her rumpled bed at the Holiday Inn. Turning onto one side, she glanced at the clock on the night table.

It read 9:20.

Alice put her nose to her blouse sleeve and sniffed.

It stank of gasoline and fire smoke.

And her face felt sunburned.

"I warned you about this business, didn't I?"

Sitting up in the other bed, propped against pillows, Dead Mary pointed a finger at Alice and then shook it sternly.

18

Ramona Pruitt left her aunt's house at twenty minutes to eleven that morning. As soon as she got into her car, she did a very uncharacteristic thing, she turned on the radio and tuned it to a local rock station. It was true what she'd told Bo last night—she *didn't* like music, at least not what she'd heard of it over the past half-dozen years. She liked dancing, but that was different. At a club, it wasn't the music that mattered, it was the blast of *sound,* and the communal energy of two hundred flailing bodies crammed together.

A lot of Ramona's friends had teased her about being so musically illiterate. They'd rattle off the names of hot new bands, best-selling albums, hit videos, and she'd just look at them blankly. Smashing Pumpkins? That was a group? Nine Inch Nails? Sorry, never heard of 'em.

Music just wasn't important to Ramona, not in the least.

So how come she was listening this morning to rock radio? And how come she paid careful, memorizing attention whenever the deejay identified a song?

Bo, she thought.

It's because of him.

He was such a sweet guy, *so* sweet that she didn't even mind that he wore a gimme cap backward; ordinarily, she hated guys who wore stupid caps, and especially she hated them if they turned their caps around. She hated that look. But on Bo—well, *his* cap looked cute. And he was so *up* all the time, so eager to please, so genuinely himself, so—

Wait a second, Ramona told herself. She hit the directional signal, eased up on the accelerator, then made a lefthand turn. You don't want to get involved with him, she thought. You really don't. He doesn't even live around here; that never works out, long-distance romance. And besides, he works in a video store. And he never finished high school. He plays guitar, for crying out loud! And he cracks his knuckles.

Yeah? So what? she immediately countered. He's a nice guy. And how many of *those* have I met recently? Bo's a nice, sweet guy, and he's crazy about me, and he doesn't know how to hide it—or show it.

I like him, she thought.

I like him a lot.

With a self-satisfied chuckle, Ramona reached out and upped the volume on the radio.

And if she had known the song that was playing, which of course she didn't, she would have sung along happily.

She expected them all to be waiting for her in the motel lobby when she arrived, but nobody was there. After standing around for a couple of minutes, Ramona decided to call upstairs. She used a courtesy phone and the operator put her through to Alice's room.

On the second ring, the cranky guy answered. (What was his name again? Spike? Ike! Ike the crank, thought Ramona.)

"Oh. Hey," said Ike. "Sorry. We're all runnin' a little bit late. 'Cause of what happened."

"Something's wrong?"

"Not really . . . wrong. Hey, why don't you just come on up?"

Ramona frowned, worried suddenly because something had "happened," and at the same time more than mildly surprised by Ike's tone of voice: he'd sounded genuinely apologetic—and friendly!

She hung up the phone and took the elevator. When the doors opened, Bo was standing there in the corridor. "Hey," he said, then grinned.

"What's going on?" Ramona asked.

"Well . . . Alice had kind of a weird experience."

"What kind of 'weird experience'?"

Bo hesitated; he seemed almost embarrassed and bit his lip. Then he shrugged, took Ramona's hand, and led her down the corridor.

"Bo? What's going on with you people? I think I deserve to know. Seeing as how I agreed to help y'all."

Alice's room door stood open.

An overpowering smell of gasoline wafted out into the corridor.

Gasoline? Ramona stopped walking—dug in her heels—and gave Bo a startled look. "I want to know what's happening. Right *now.*"

"I'm really not sure."

"Bo!"

"Okay," he said finally in a faltering tone. "All right. Do you believe in ghosts?"

"I'm not really—what are you *saying? Ghosts?*"

"Alice saw one this morning." He squeezed gently on her hand. "*That's* what going on."

Fletch, Alice, and Ike turned and nodded simultaneously when Ramona came into the room. But then they all glanced back at the newspaper spread open in front of them.

Bo said, "I think you should have a look at that," and led Ramona to the desk. Fletch stepped aside, allowing her a clear view of the newspaper.

It was the *Richmond News-Leader.*

Dated Thursday, May 17, 1934.

The paper, though, wasn't yellowed in the least. It seemed as white and as crisp as yesterday's edition—although there wouldn't have *been* any edition yesterday, since the *News-Leader* was no longer published.

"Where did you find this?" Ramona asked.

Alice said, "A woman named Mary Dunham gave it to me."

"Mary Dunham?"

"That's, um, the ghost I was telling you about," said Bo.

"People? Are you all nuts? What's going on here? You think you could—?"

Ike jabbed a finger against the newspaper. "Ramona? Don't worry about ghosts, all right? Forget that. Just look at this!"

Ramona's gaze traveled to where Ike's finger was pointing, and what she saw made her catch her breath.

The headline read: ORPHAN FIRES STILL A MYSTERY.

"That's—"

"What your aunt was telling us about last night. Exactly," said Fletch.

"And that same guy is mentioned," said Ike. "That Thomas Dunbar Lawrence guy. The guy Jude Hayser asked you if you'd ever heard of."

Pressing her palms flat on the desktop, Ramona leaned over the paper and began reading the article: dozens of tents burned, no bodies, no trace of the orphans—the scores of orphans—who'd mysteriously gathered in the field two weeks earlier.

Basically, it was the same story Aunt Ardeth had summarized for them.

But there was one interesting—very interesting—new detail. The news article surmised that most of the missing orphans, who ranged in age from sixteen or seventeen to their early twenties, had all been sent, years earlier, on special trains from orphanages in Boston, New York, Newark, and Philadelphia to little towns in the South and the Midwest. At each train stop they'd been herded onto the station platform, where local farmers, shop owners, mill owners, and horse breeders had looked them over, checked their muscles and their teeth, then "adopted" one or two, or several.

"Some adoptions," Ramona murmured. "It sounds like these poor kids were being sold as slaves."

"Yeah," said Ike, "except they didn't *cost* anything. They came absolutely free."

Ramona nodded, then continued to read the article. Suddenly she laughed, darkly. "Did you see this quote?" Then she read out loud: " 'Charles City County Sheriff Horace

Kitts declined to speculate about the whereabouts of the young men and women missing from Hobart Hayser's tobacco farm. "It sure is peculiar," he said, "but I don't think anybody needs to lose too much sleep over it. These people weren't from around here. And besides," added Sheriff Kitts, "they was just orphans." ' "

Ramona shook her head in disgust. "Just orphans," she said. "Reminds me of that old Woody Guthrie song—you know it? The one called 'Plane Crash at Los Gatos'? It's about these Mexican migrant workers who were being flown back home as illegal aliens. Well, their plane crashed in the California mountains and they were all killed, and the radio announcer who reported the story said they were all 'just deportees.' As if it didn't really matter that they died, 'cause they just weren't *important*. And Woody Guthrie got so angry when he heard that, he put it into a song."

Bo was staring at Ramona with complete mystification. And undisguised adoration. He said, "I thought you didn't like music?"

"Well . . . it's an *old* song."

"That's cool. I got nothing against old songs. I don't know it, but I'm gonna make it my business to hear it someday. What's the name of it again?"

Before Ramona could respond, Ike said, "Hey, can you guys talk about this some other time?"

"Sorry," said Ramona. "I just . . . the comment by that stupid sheriff, it got to me. 'They was just orphans.' Man! People sure could be heartless in the old days."

"Oh, and you think they're not now?" asked Ike.

"Look," Fletch interjected, "this is a fascinating conversation, but we really should get a move on, huh?"

Alice picked up the old newspaper and closed it, folded it in half, and stuck it into her bag. "Yeah," she said. "Let's go visit Jude Hayser." She looked pale and her voice was hushed. Her hands, Ramona noticed, were trembling slightly.

"Alice?" Ramona touched her on the arm. "I'm still in the

dark about what went on here this morning. How you got that paper and—"

"I was *there*," Alice said, looking directly into Ramona's face.

"Where?"

"At Hayser's farm that night. In May of 1934. Somehow, I . . . got there. Don't ask me how, but I saw everybody go into their tents. I saw the tents being set on fire. And I saw . . . him. Thomas Dunbar Lawrence." Alice smiled suddenly. "You don't believe me? Then how come I smell like freakin' gasoline? And how come my face is scorched and my eyebrows are singed? I was *there*, Ramona, I swear to God. *I saw it!*"

Ramona moistened her lips. Her expression was cautious, still doubtful.

"And Mary Dunham's ghost saved my life," said Alice. "She pulled me out of there before I got burned to a crisp. And she gave me this—" Alice tapped the newspaper in her bag—"just so I'd know for sure where I'd been."

Ramona threw up her hands in exasperation. "If you say so! But I have to tell you, I'm starting to believe what everybody down here says about Yankees. You're all as crazy as bedbugs."

"Ah, we're not that bad," said Bo.

"Oh, yes we are," Fletch said, then he laughed gruffly as he moved toward the open doorway. "Alice didn't tell you, Ramona, but Mary Dunham charged her twenty-five bucks for the rescue. Even Yankee *ghosts* are as crazy as bedbugs!"

19

Ike was beginning to suspect that Ramona Pruitt was a
Queen Ditz. Already she'd mistakenly identified three different cutoff roads as the one leading into Jude Hayser's
property. "No, this isn't it," she said each time, wincing as
she apologized. "Must be a little farther along." And Alice
had to turn the van around, nose it carefully back out onto
Route 5, and keep going east, heading toward Williamsburg.

It was a few minutes past one o'clock in the afternoon,
they'd been on the road nearly forty-five minutes.

"Jeez," said Ramona, "I didn't think it was *this* far."

And Ike said, "Uh-huh."

Now, as she bounced once again off her seat in the back,
lunged forward and tapped Alice on the shoulder, Ike pushed
out his lips and rolled his eyes. "This is it!" she cried. "This
is it!"

"You sure?" he asked.

"I'm sure! Alice—pull over!"

Alice did, then steered the van, but slowly and very carefully, up the narrow, gullied dirt track. Branches scraped
and ticked against the sides. Stones ricocheted off the
undercarriage.

When the open field, the distant slate-gray river, and the
old farmhouse and its barn finally came into view, Alice
stepped on the brake. She turned, glancing at Fletch seated
in back with Bo and Ramona. "Should I drive to the house?"

"Of course!" Ike answered before Fletch could, positively
annoyed that she asked *him* at all. Who put Fletch in charge
of operations? "We go straight to the house," he continued,
"then we knock on the door, and then we—"

"—act like decent human beings when we finally meet

91

this guy," said Fletch. "You got that, Ikey? We don't barge in, we don't play tough, and we definitely do not accuse him of *anything*. 'Cause guess what? We don't know for sure that he *did* anything. We just ask about Del. Got that? Unless, of course, you want to blow it all right now and maybe get ourselves arrested to boot. For trespassing. You following me?"

Ike felt his muscles grow tense. His shoulders rose, and he gritted his teeth. He didn't turn around, though. Nor did he reply.

"You *following* me?"

"Up yours, Fletch," he said then, in a strained voice. "And don't ever call me Ikey. *Ever.*"

"What's with you two guys?" asked Bo. "Calm down, already. Jeez." When he looked at Ramona next to him, she had that apprehensive you're-all-are-as-crazy-as-bedbugs expression in her eyes again. He patted her hand, and she smiled.

"Okay, then," said Alice, "we drive right up to the front door." Drawing a deep breath and letting it out slowly, she tapped the accelerator, and the van rolled forward.

"Hey! That house? Reminds me of the one in *Psycho*," Bo said. "Except, like, it's not on top of a hill."

Fletch shook his head. "Gotta hand it to you, kid. You always know just the right thing to say."

Ike had barely heard that last exchange. He was in too much turmoil now to pay much attention to the others. In fact, it took most of his powers of concentration just to keep his hands flat on his thighs; otherwise they would've snapped into angry fists. He was so impatient to find out whether or not Del was in that old farmhouse up ahead—either as a guest or as a prisoner—that he almost jumped from the van and sprinted there.

But he held himself in check. And made himself inhale and exhale normally. Inhale. Exhale. Inhale. Exhale. . . .

It was galling for Ike to realize how well, and how accurately, Fletch had read his intentions. He *had* planned to come on strong and hostile with this Jude Hayser when they finally met. Strong, hostile, and accusatory. But Ike now had to admit to himself (and this was even more galling) that Fletch was right to caution him against playing it that way.

So let's just do it nice and easy. For now.

Inhale, he thought.

Exhale.

Alice parked outside the slouching, paint-scabbed white picket fence that surrounded the front yard of the Hayser farmhouse. After switching off the ignition and setting the hand brake, she half-turned in her seat and met her brother's eyes levelly.

"So," she said. "What're you waiting for?"

"Nothing," he replied with a quick grin then rolled out of the van before the others, flicked up the hook on the fence gate, and practically ran across the yard. He took the porch steps two at a time and, before the others were even through the gate, he was knocking at the door.

Knocking, not pounding.

There was no response, so he tried the doorknob.

Locked.

"Maybe he's out back," Ramona suggested. "Where I found him last time."

"Whyn't you and Bo go check?" said Ike, and he knocked again. Then he cupped his hands to a sidelight and peered into the house.

All he could see (and see dimly, since the glass was filthy) was a plank-floored central hallway, and another door—a door leading to the backyard—at the end of it.

"Hayser!" Ike suddenly bellowed, and started walloping the flat of his hand against the door, as hard as he could. "Jude Hayser!"

Fletch laid a cautioning hand on his shoulder. "I don't think he's home, Ike."

"I do." Then, "Hayser! Jude Hayser!"

"Nobody in the back," Bo called. He came drifting around

the side of the house with Ramona. "So what do we do now?"

With a half-shrug, Fletch turned to Alice. "We could wait, I guess. Or come back later."

"He's *here*," said Ike. "I *know* he's here! And if he doesn't come out, then all bets are off—and I'm breaking in."

"Oh, no, you're not," said Fletch.

"He's here!"

"Well, he's not answering the damn door, is he?" said Alice. "So all you're doing is making a lot of noise and giving *me* a headache, so why don't you just quit it? *Quit it!*"

Ike froze, startled by his sister's angry outburst.

"Thank you," Alice said quietly. "Let's all just . . . think for a second." She walked back down the porch steps. Then, glancing off to her right and narrowing her eyes, she pointed suddenly. "Somebody should look in there."

The barn. It stood canted, wobbly, with boards missing from the side walls and large, gaping holes in the shingled roof.

"We'll do it," said Ramona, taking Bo's hand and leading him across the yard past a thick-trunked oak tree that had an old rain-filled tire-swing dangling from a branch by a frayed rope.

Meanwhile, Ike had recommenced banging on the door. "Hayser!" he called. "Hayser! Jude Hayser!"

Alice rolled her eyes. But suddenly her uplifted gaze focused on a small, round attic window.

Her heart lurched.

The window in the photograph!

It was! It was the attic window in the photograph!

Or was it?

Maybe it was just . . . similar.

She was about to call Fletch over, to show it to him and see what he thought, when Bo yelled from the barn. "Hey! You guys! C'mere! C'mere and look at this!"

Even Ike came.

"I *told* you I seen that guy in an old sixties junker," Bo said, with a showman's flourish.

Ike shoved past Fletch and Alice and stepped inside the barn. Through chinks in the roof, daylight flecked with chaff and billions of dust particles beamed down in skinny, criss-crossing shafts. Rats squeaked in the hayloft. "You said it was a Ford, Bo. That's a Plymouth."

"I said *maybe* a Ford. What do I know from cars? And what's it matter—*that's* the car. That's the car I seen him sitting in, when Del said she wasn't coming back with us to Jersey. This baby right here." And he kicked the front side tire.

Spattered with dried mud, flecked all over with scabs of bright rust, the tires bald, and the radio antenna replaced by a wire coat hanger, the faded green thirty-year-old Plymouth stood parked in the aisle between empty horse stalls. On the red-dirt floor, irregular blots of motor oil made Rorschach patterns.

Pulling open the driver's door, Ike leaned into the car. Then he slid under the wheel, reached over, opened the glove compartment and snooped for a moment. Slammed it shut.

"What're you looking for?" It was Fletch, hanging on the open driver's door.

"I don't know. something of hers. When Del split from you guys, what'd she take with her?"

"Just the clothes she had on. And that little bag she always carries. Her wallet. That stuff."

"And her magic book," Bo added. "You know the one we were talking about? With the spell in it so you don't get a speeding ticket?"

"She took that?" said Ike.

"Uh-huh."

Ike thought a moment, then reached a hand under the driver's seat and felt around. Then he felt around under the front passenger's seat. He peered over into the back.

Except for a greasy auto mechanic's bill from 1991, he found absolutely nothing.

When he got out of the Plymouth, Ike slammed the door angrily. "Well, here's his car. Didn't I tell you he was in that house? And I don't care *what* you say, Fletch, I'm going back over there now and I'm gonna kick in that freakin' door."

"Oh, I don't think so," said a drawling voice from the direction of the barn door. "I really don't think you're going to do that at all."

The young man was pale, tall, angular, and gaunt, and dressed entirely in black. Black shirt, black jean jacket, black riveted jeans, black sneakers.

Even the revolver in his grip was black.

20

"Ah don't like having a weapon pointed at me, sir, if you don't mind!" said Ramona Pruitt, sounding very cross, very steely, and—bless her heart, thought Bo, she's laying it on—very, very Southern.

The man in black was obviously startled to see her. He gaped at her now as she broke away from the group huddled beside the Plymouth and crossed the barn, moving forward without hesitation or any token of nervousness.

"So, Mr. Jude Hayser, would you kindly put that dangerous thing away?"

He said, "Mona? What're *you* doing here?"

"First, that goes."

Jude Hayser glanced at his revolver, smiled weakly, then lowered his right arm to his side. "You're trespassin'," he said. "All of you." He narrowed his eyes, glaring at Ramona. "You included."

"Well, if you say so, Jude Hayser. But let me just tell you something. We came out here to talk to you—"

"Talk? That fellow over there—" he nodded crisply toward Ike—"wanted to kick in my front door!"

"Only because you wouldn't answer it when he knocked."

"I didn't hear any knocking."

"Foo," said Ramona, and Bo (standing behind Fletch and ready to duck if that gun jerked up again) was so startled by her expression that he barked out a laugh.

Foo?

"You heard us," said Ramona. "But you didn't want to answer. You're just an old . . . hermit!"

"I don't intend to argue with you, Mona Pruitt. I said I didn't hear you, and that's the case. I didn't. I was sleeping."

"At one-thirty on a beautiful Sunday afternoon?"

"Mona, you're startin' to annoy me. But, yes—at one-thirty on a beautiful Sunday. I ... I haven't been feeling well. Not that it's any of your business."

Ike stepped forward then. "Well, now that you mention our business—"

"And who the hell are you?" Instinctively, Jude's gun hand began to rise.

Ike made a spare, placating gesture. "My name's Ike Fuelle. And this is my sister Alice. And these are my friends. And I wasn't *really* gonna kick in your door. Honest." A smile flickered on his face, then steadied till it looked one-hundred-percent genuine. And politely friendly.

Alice thought, Sometimes—not often, but sometimes— I'm proud to be that guy's sister.

"You probably can tell from the way I talk that I'm not from around here, Mr. Hayser," Ike continued. "None of us is, except for Ramona, who's been kind enough to help us out."

"Help you out doing what, exactly?" Jude asked.

"Well, sir," said Ike (and Alice nearly plopped, she'd never heard him address anybody as "sir" before, never), "we came all the way down here from New Jersey because—"

"New Jersey?" said Jude Hayser. "Do you know Del Scho-field? Is *she* with you?" Leaning slightly to his left, he peered past Ike at the others standing beside the Plymouth in the dim recess of the barn.

Ike's jaw dropped open. For a long moment, he was utterly confused.

Finally, "No, she's ... well, see, that's how come we came out here to see you. We thought that maybe *you'd* know where she was."

"Me?" said Jude Hayser. "Why would *I* know where she is? Truth be told, though, I'd love to see her again. I liked that girl a lot. I surely did."

Ike felt as if the barn floor was suddenly rolling—rump-ling—beneath him and would, at any moment, crack open in a gaping fissure to swallow him up.

He said, "When, um, did you see her last?"

"I gather that Del is missing?" said Jude Hayser.

"Yeah, she's . . ." Ike looked frantically over his shoulder at Fletch and Alice, pleading without words for them to step in and help him out. Because right then, he didn't know what else to say.

Although Ike couldn't remember much about his parents very clearly, he did remember a pet expression of his mother's. She used to say—and Ike couldn't imagine why, exactly— "Well! That certainly took the wind out of your sails!" Which is what Jude Hayser's comments about Del had suddenly done to Ike. Taken the wind out of his sails. Completely. Utterly.

Alice moved away from the Plymouth and stood beside her brother. She touched his wrist (affectionately, or perhaps con- solingly), then she turned a forlorn smile toward Jude Hayser. "Del never came home," said Alice. "And it's two weeks today. So. Well. You can imagine how worried we've been."

"Home?" said Jude Hayser. "She lives with *you*?"

"She has been—why do you ask?"

Jude shook his head. "No reason." He looked at his re- volver again, then jammed it into the waistband of his jeans. "But why did you all think I'd know where she was?"

"Because," said Fletch, stepping forward, "we saw you with Del at the Moon Lamp and then again the next day on Brown's Island. So we figured . . ."

Jude Hayser nodded. "I see." He finally allowed himself a tiny smile. "And on the basis of that, you all naturally figured that I'd kidnapped her and killed her and chopped her up and buried her on my property. I get it."

Fletch said, "No, that's not what we—"

Jude cut him off with a swiftly raised hand. "Well, at least you *suspected* as much. No need to be so defensive, though. I probably would have felt the same thing myself, if I were you-all."

There was a long silence.

Then, "I wish I could help," said Jude Hayser, "but I haven't seen Del since—well, that Sunday afternoon. She wanted to get a little tour of Richmond, so I volunteered and drove her around for a couple of hours."

"And then?. . ." said Ike.

"Then we had lunch—"

"Where?"

"Some little place on Cary Street. And then I dropped her back at the Moon Lamp."

"You did? When was this?"

"Early Sunday evening."

"Why'd she want to go back there?"

"To listen to music, I suppose. I really can't say."

"But," Alice said, "did she tell you where she intended to *stay* that night?"

"No."

"And you didn't ask her?"

"I thought that might be . . . inappropriate. I was afraid that she might think that I was trying to—well, I just thought it would be indelicate to pry into her business. After all, we'd only just met." He smiled thinly. "And that's the last I saw of her. We had a very nice afternoon, and that was that." His gaze flicked from Ike to Alice to Fletch. "I wish I could be of more help to you all, but I . . . don't know anything more than what I've just told you."

Ike's hands felt like ice, and it seemed as if there were a hole the size of a cannonball in his stomach, through which a freezing wind was blowing.

Now what? he thought. *Now* what?

"Thank you, Jude," said Ramona. "Sorry we had to bother you, but you've been real helpful. And it's nice seein' you again."

"Likewise," said Jude. Then, with a general nod—a nod to all in the barn—he turned and walked out through the ten-foot-high double doors. Ike noticed that he staggered a little. And seemed very weak. But was that surprising? No. The man in black was abnormally thin, as thin as a rail. To look at him, you'd think he was starving to death.

"We should go, too," said Ramona.

In mutual gloom, everyone filed outside into the sunlight.

21

On the drive into Richmond, nobody said anything—nobody felt much like talking.

For days now, they'd assumed that the key to Del Schofield's disappearance was the mysterious Orphan Jude. Find him and they'd find her. Simple as that. But now that they had found him, actually had found and spoken with him, they were no closer—not a smidgen closer—to discovering what really had happened to their friend.

And now it was late Sunday afternoon, and they had to decide whether or not to drive back home this evening.

Give it up?

Give it all up?

"You know someplace good to eat?" Alice asked Ramona. "We should have some food and talk about what we're gonna do next."

"Someplace good and *cheap*," said Bo. "My funds are running low."

"Yeah, sure," Ramona said. "There's a little diner just a few blocks from your motel on Second Street."

So that's where they ended up ten minutes later. Ramona knew all the wait staff (she'd worked there the past summer), so they got a corner booth and prompt service. But when their sandwiches, fries, and Cokes or coffee came, the plates and glasses remained untouched. Nobody was hungry. Nobody was thirsty. Nobody was happy.

"I guess—" Alice started, then shook her head and shrugged.

"What?" said Ike. "You guess what?"

"I guess we have to decide a few things. First, are we going home tonight?"

"No, wait. Even before that," said Ike, "we should decide something else. Do we believe anything that Jude Hayser told us? Fletch?"

"He seemed . . . okay. I don't know. The one thing that got to me? When Alice said that Del lived with you guys—it surprised him. Like he thought she was, what? Homeless? A drifter?"

"An orphan?" said Alice.

"Yeah, I caught that, too," said Bo. "But is it a big deal?"

"Maybe not," said Fletch. "But something else strikes me funny. What do you think it was about Del that a guy like Jude Hayser would find so . . . likable? I don't know about you, but he didn't seem the sort who'd dig girls with spiked-out hair."

"And what about Del?" said Ike. "Why would she want to spend time with him? And why the heck would she want a tour of Richmond? Sightseeing is definitely not her thing."

Bo shrugged. "What *I* was thinking . . ."

Everybody looked at him expectantly.

"This Jude, right? Said that he dropped Del off at The Moon Lamp. But Mouse said he never seen her again after Saturday night. So, like, either *he's* lying . . . or Jude is. One or the other."

"Unless Mouse wasn't there Sunday night," said Fletch.

"We could check," Ike said.

Bo suddenly leaned forward and picked up his sandwich (pork barbecue, on Ramona's recommendation). He opened his mouth to take a bite, then frowned and put it back down on the plate. "Any of you guys notice how *skinny* that Jude dude was? Man! He looked like he hadn't eaten for weeks!" Bo pinched a sesame seed off the bun, then vacuum-sucked it into his mouth. "Or maybe he's just—what's that word? Microbiotic."

"Macrobiotic," Ramona said. "And I don't think so. Not Jude. But I noticed myself how skinny he'd gotten."

"*Gotten?*" said Ike. "You mean he wasn't like that last month?"

"He was thin, but . . . but he didn't look like he was going to blow over in the first breeze."

They all fell silent again, thinking their own thoughts and staring communally at the untouched food and drink on the table.

Across the aisle from their booth, two guys dressed in gym sweats dropped coins into a wall-mounted mini-jukebox and punched in their selections.

Moments later, R.E.M.'s "Losing My Religion" started playing.

Ike Fuelle gritted his teeth. Del, he thought bitterly, could have been just as big as those guys, bigger. She could have had *her* picture on the cover of *Rolling Stone* and *Spin*. She could have been on MTV. Could have . . .

Abruptly, he stood up. "I gotta go get some fresh air."

"Wait a second, Ikey," said Alice.

"Ike! *Ike!* How many times I gotta tell you, it's—"

"I'm sorry. Okay? Really. But don't leave yet. Please? We gotta decide if we're going home tonight."

"I think we *have* to, Alice," said Fletch. "I've got work tomorrow, Bo's got work, you've got the store . . ."

"Then go home, you guys," said Ike. "But I'm staying."

He tossed down a five-dollar bill, smiled so-long at Ramona, nodded vaguely at the others, then left the diner. He scuttled past waiters and customers, the corners of his eyes tingling; feeling light-headed with loss, apprehension, and despair.

22

After leaving the Second Street Diner, Ike wandered aimlessly with his hands plunged into his pockets and his eyes fixed morosely on the pavement. Damn, he thought at one point, the others are right—we *should* all go home tonight. What's there left to do here? If Jude Hayser was telling the truth, then Del could be—anywhere.

Anywhere.

If he was telling the truth.

"Hey, pal? Spare some change?"

Ike glanced up at an emaciated, gray-faced man with clumps of dirt-caked black hair sticking up and out from his head. Dressed in a frayed corduroy sport jacket, crusty blue slacks, and a pair of heavy workboots, he was leaning against a lamppost several feet away. Accompanied by a well-practiced, pitiable smile, he extended a begging hand.

Ike pulled out whatever small change he had in his pocket—a few quarters, but mostly nickels and pennies—and dropped everything, clinking softly, into the man's palm. Without giving his meager booty even a glance, the man snapped his hand closed, nodded vaguely, muttered "God bless you" with an edge of scorn to his voice, then pushed off from the lamppost and clomped heavily away.

Now that the beggar had gone, Ike saw that he'd been leaning against one of the flyers they'd taped up around the city.

HAVE YOU SEEN THIS GIRL?

Ike stepped closer to it and stared for a minute at Del's photograph.

Where *are* you? he thought.

Shaking his head, he turned away, then stopped.

The flyers!

All of them had Alice's name and the motel's phone number printed on them—but so far, nobody had thought to check the front desk for any messages!

Ike glanced around for a street sign to get his bearings. And when he determined that the Holiday Inn was just one block north and two blocks east, he took off running.

The attendant at the registration desk that late Sunday afternoon was a slender woman in her middle forties, and when Ike suddenly burst into the lobby, she looked alarmed, enough to push a concealed button and alert the police. Fortunately, he recognized the look in her eye and forced himself to slow down. By the time he'd reached the desk, he was walking at a normal pace and smiling like an Eagle Scout.

"May I—help you?" asked the woman.

"Any calls for Room Three-Twelve? Any messages?"

"You're a guest here?"

"Yes, ma'am," he replied.

To Ike, his saying "ma'am" instantly made the conversation seem like total make-believe—corny dialogue in a scene between a cowboy and a schoolmarm in an old John Wayne picture. But it did the trick: The desk clerk's mouth turned up and she asked, "What was that room again, sir?"

"Three-Twelve."

She turned and grazed her eyes over a wall of cubbies, each one identified by a number engraved on a brass oval beneath it. Reaching into cubby 312, she retrieved several square slips of pink paper. Ike had to restrain himself from snatching them from her hand.

"Thanks a lot," he told her, quickly counting the messages (four!), and then adding, "ma'am."

As he took the elevator up, he finally permitted himself a glance at the messages. All of them had been phoned in during the afternoon, but none came with a name, just a local number to call.

Wait a second, somebody had phoned twice.

So there were only three messages, really. Oh, well, three were still . . . three.

Ike hurried along the empty corridor. Dipping a laminated key-card into the lock, he opened his door, stepped inside, and flicked up the light switch. Then he practically dove for the telephone.

As he was dialing the first number, though, he realized that he didn't have anything to write with. Or on. He hung up and searched for a pad and pen—and naturally couldn't find either.

He went into Alice's room by the connecting door.

There he found several sheets of lined white paper and a couple of pens lying on the desk, alongside the photograph of the white tent in the gloomy attic.

Carefully, he tapped in the first phone number.

Someone answered on the fourth ring. A man's voice.

"My name is Ike Fuelle—you called me this afternoon?"

"I'm sorry, you must have the wrong number. I don't know anybody named—"

"I think you probably called a number that you saw on a flyer. About a missing girl?"

"Oh yes! Yes, I did call. Your name again?"

"Ike."

"Well, Ike, it's like this. I was out walking my dog this morning when I saw your little flyer, and the moment I did, well, sir, I recognized that face. I surely, surely did! Never forget it."

"Uh-huh," said Ike, surprised to discover that he was having trouble breathing. His throat felt constricted and his heart raced. "And could you tell me exactly *where* you saw Del? And when?"

"Del?"

"That's her name: Del. Del Schofield."

"In my backyard, young man. I saw her in my own backyard. Well, first of course, I saw the lights. Blinding blue lights. And when I looked outside, there she was, standing right under those beams. Then the ship took her up."

"Ship?"

"The mother-ship. Oh, it was a great big thing, so beautiful! Then a shaft of yellow light beamed down, and up she went. Up she went! And then that old mother-ship just zoomed away! Big as it was, it could turn on a dime, young man. Just turn on a thin dime!"

Ike hung up.

The second caller was just as loopy. Loopier. A woman who'd seen Del at Hollywood Cemetery, walking after midnight with the shades of James Madison, Jefferson Davis, and Edgar Allan Poe.

By the time he got off the phone with that nutcase, Ike was so dispirited he almost crumpled up the final two message slips, the ones with the same phone number. But he made himself place the call. For Del's sake.

Four rings, then an answering machine clicked on: "Hi! You've reached the home of Greg Odet. Sorry that I'm not here right now, but if you'll leave your name and a brief message, I'll get back to you just as soon as I can. Thanks for calling—and you have a great day, all right?"

Ike hated leaving messages on recording machines—he always stammered, corrected himself, rambled, and generally sounded dumb and disorganized; he *hated* those suckers!—so without waiting for the beep, he replaced the receiver in the cradle. Then he sat on the side of Alice's bed, trying to think why the name Greg Odet rang a bell.

Who, besides Mouse Mineo, did he know in Richmond, Virginia?

Greg Odet, Greg Odet. . . .

Ike braced his elbows on his knees, pressed his fingertips against his forehead, and racked his brains.

Greg Odet. . . .

Finally, he quit trying to remember. And since five minutes had passed since he'd placed the last call, he dialed the number again. But he just got the same hearty message again.

Fed up, discouraged anew, Ike made a fist, pounded the

mattress, then forced himself to his feet. You know what? he thought. I'm going home. I am. I'm going home with everybody else tonight. And the hell with all this!

As he was crossing the room to the connecting door, he paused, then glanced back at the desk. He walked over and stood staring intently at the photograph.

A white tent. Pitched in an attic. Daylight seeping through chinks in the roof, streaming through a small medallion window.

Snapping the photo back down onto the desk, Ike pivoted around, snatched up the telephone, and dialed New Jersey Information.

A minute later he was speaking with Danny Dunham. "Ike Fuelle? My goodness, this is a surprise! How are you, Ike? And how's your sis—"

"I need to talk to your mother, Danny. Right now."

"I'm sorry, but Mother is napping. But I'll certainly tell her that you called."

"Not good enough! I want to talk to her! This morning she dropped by to see Alice—"

"Oh, I hardly think so, Ike. Mother hasn't been out of the house all day."

"Danny, please! She gave Alice a picture the other day, and I have to know more about it. I have to! This is an emergency!"

"I'll tell Mother that you called. When she wakes up," said Danny Dunham, then he broke the connection.

Ike clenched his hand around the receiver like it was a war club. Oh, go write a poem, you old nerd, he thought. He felt boiled up enough to throw a violent tantrum—to smash the receiver against the wall—but he finally got control of himself. Drawing a deep breath, holding it, feeling all of his pulse points throb, he carefully hung up the telephone.

This *isn't* a wild goose chase, he thought.

We're close. Very close.

If we could just . . .

If *I* could just . . .

He went over and picked up the photo again. Brought it closer to his face, so near that his vision gradually lost focus.

Suddenly, the hair crisped on the back of Ike's neck, and a wave of blistering heat slammed his face.

A moment later, he was totally engulfed by red-and-yellow flames.

Just the way he'd dreamed it, all those times.

Only this time it was really happening.

23

Wildly, Ike slapped at his clothes, at his hair, as flames and fiery strips of airborne canvas whirled around him. Black smoke ballooned so thick that he couldn't see or breathe. And no matter how hard Ike insisted in a screeching mind-voice that this couldn't be real, couldn't be happening, the firestorm roared around him, growing louder, and his flesh began to blister. His lungs were shutting down. Someplace not far away, dogs were barking in terror.

And now, pressing a forearm against his mouth and nostrils, Ike stumbled forward through grass that charred his sneakers and singed his jeans. On both sides of him, blazing tents were disintegrating, bursting apart, collapsing; guylines snapped and flew off like glowing snakes.

Afraid that he'd blunder directly into a wall of flames, Ike forced his eyes open into slits that tingled and watered.

Directly ahead of him, he spotted a fire-free area. He ran for it, but as he did, smoke closed around him again. He kept running. The smoke lifted briefly, long enough for him to confirm that he was still headed for the open, unconsumed part of the field.

Then he saw it. Another tent, set off by itself.

And not burning.

Smoke roiled up once more, surrounding him, and Ike felt his lungs rebel. His body became wracked by a series of gasping, wrenching coughs. He went dizzy—his conscious mind started to break up and flitter away. He shook his head to clear it, then staggered on.

He could see that white tent again, perhaps twenty feet ahead of him now.

And a man!

He could see a tall, terribly thin man, dressed in ministerial black—frock coat, dark shirt, dark trousers, dark shoes—hastily undoing the tie-tapes that held the tent flaps together.

Ike tried to call out, but as soon as he opened his mouth, he swallowed a lungful of hot, black smoke, and was choking again, barking 'hectic' coughs.

The tall man glanced around. When he spotted Ike, his eyes grew wide with astonishment.

For just a moment it seemed as if he meant to signal Ike forward. His left hand, fingers crooked, lifted briefly in a tentative, beckoning gesture. But then, as another gust of smoke blew in laterally, carrying with it pin-dot sparks and tatters of burning fabric that settled on, or glanced across the last standing tent, the tall man—with an expression of grave alarm—suddenly turned his back on Ike. He parted the entrance flaps and ducked inside.

Seconds later, his tent's sloped roof caught fire in a half-dozen places.

Ike made himself charge ahead, chuffing like a seventy-year-old man who's smoked a billion cigarettes in his lifetime. His vision began to swim. When he was just several feet from the tent, he found the strength to croak weakly. "Mister," he said, "you gotta get out of there!" The effort almost sapped his last reserve of strength.

As Ike reached a hand toward the tent, somebody—hurtling in from his left side—whacked it away. "Mine!" came a voice. "Find your own darn souvenir!"

It was a boy, lanky, beanpole-thin, about fourteen, with a long, narrow face, deep-set hostile eyes, and straight oil-black hair He was dressed in denim coveralls, and carried a folded green army blanket.

Without another glance at Ike, the boy snapped the blanket open. Holding it by one corner and bunched tightly in a fist, he brandished it like a whip and savagely beat out the flames nibbling the tall man's tent.

As soon as they all were extinguished, the boy gave a feral whoop of triumph. Then, as Ike watched in amazement, he

111

ran gleefully around the tent, yanking up its stakes, one after the other.

Poles wobbling beneath white canvas, the tent began to fold in on itself.

But where was the tall man?

Ike had seen him duck inside a minute ago!

With the tent now lying crumpled on the ground, the young boy dropped to his knees and quickly rolled it up into a large bundle. It took only a few seconds, and when he was finished, he tied it around with stake lines.

Then he began dragging it across the field, away from the fires.

"Hey!" Ike called. "Hey!"

But it was as if the boy didn't hear him.

"Hey!"

Ike had been so fascinated (and for some unaccountable reason, repulsed) by the sight of the strange dark-haired farm-boy attacking and dismantling the white tent that he'd forgotten to pay any attention to the conflagration behind him. Now, though, he felt a painful blast of heat. Turning, he confronted a maw of raging, barbed fire twice his height. It fell upon him and swallowed him up entirely.

24

When Ike never returned to the diner, Alice first became annoyed, then angry, and finally worried sick.

They'd waited for him nearly an hour—drinking coffee, having dessert, having a second dessert, drinking more coffee. Fletch, at last, had waited long enough. "Let's go back to our rooms, okay? Your nutso brother is probably there anyhow," he said.

But he wasn't.

Though he'd certainly *been* there, and recently.

It was Bo who spotted the phone-message slips lying on the night table in Alice's room.

"Maybe . . ." said Ramona, then stopped.

"Maybe what?" asked Alice.

Ramona shrugged.

"I bet you he called these phone numbers," said Bo. "And I bet you that he went to meet somebody who seen Del."

"Without telling us first?" Alice snatched up the four pink slips of paper, looked them over quickly, and frowned. "I don't think he'd do that."

Fletch craned an eyebrow. He, on the other hand, thought Ike was capable of doing precisely that. The little jerk. "Could I have a look at those?" he asked Alice, reaching for the slips. Then he picked up the phone and dialed the number on the top one.

Everybody watched him anxiously.

Fletch cupped a hand over the mouthpiece. "Answering machine," he said. Then he cocked his head quizzically.

"What?" said Alice. "What?"

"Ramona," said Fletch. "That realtor, the one you met at Jude's farm. What was his name?"

"Greg—"

Fletch held up one finger for silence, then said, "Mr. Odet? My name is Steve Fletcher, I believe you called about a flyer we put up around town. If you could get back to me as soon as you can, I'd appreciate it. Thank you."

He hung up, then gazed down at the telephone for half a minute. When he looked up at last, Alice, Bo, and Ramona were all staring open-mouthed at him.

"Greg Odet called about the flyer?" said Ramona.

"Apparently. Why *else* would he call us?"

Fletch plopped down heavily on the side of Alice's bed. "You know what I think?" he asked, looking directly at Alice.

"Of course I know what you think. If Greg Odet saw Del, then he saw her at Jude Hayser's farm. Otherwise it's just too crazy a coincidence."

Fletch nodded. "Yeah, that's what I think. But we'd better sit tight and wait for him to tell us that himself."

"Do you think he already told Ike?"

"It's possible. But if you're afraid that he went out to the farm by himself, relax, kiddo. He didn't. He couldn't. We've got the van—remember? And he sure as heck didn't walk there."

"So where *is* he?"

Fletch shook his head.

Suddenly, "Oh, my God!" cried Ramona. "Look!"

On top of the desk, the white-tent photograph had burst spontaneously into flames, its edges blackening as they curled slowly inward.

Then the telephone rang.

25

"I guess I should thank you."

"You *guess*?"

"All right, I should. Thank you," Ike said.

"You're welcome," said Dead Mary. When she saw that he was about to stand up from his chair, she made a quick, irritable hand gesture, and he lowered himself again—very slowly. "That's better. Now, Dwight, perhaps you'll tell me why you felt it necessary to telephone my house. Daniel thought you sounded frantic."

"It's Ike. Not Dwight."

Dead Mary smiled without mirth. "It's Dwight, boy. I don't see any charm in shortening a person's given name. And I don't believe in nicknames, either. I never have. So, then, Dwight, please answer my question. Why did you call me earlier?"

"The photograph."

"That's not a question—that's an article and a noun."

Ike pinched his bottom lip, pulled on it, then let it snap back against his front teeth. He stared for a long moment at Dead Mary, sitting beside him propped up in her enormous bed. Then he scowled and glanced over a shoulder, his gaze tracking across the farm field.

Several hundred yards away, the tent bivouac was smoldering now. Here and there, grass patches continued to burn. From several directions, men and women were running toward the fire site, or were standing around it, pointing. He could hear startled, quizzical, confused voices, all of them raised, and the resonant clang-clang-clang of an approaching fire truck.

Silhouetted at the far edge of the field stood a farmhouse. Ike recognized it. Hayser's. It was Jude Hayser's house.

This is nuts, he thought. I'm sitting in a chair next to a bed in an open field. Speaking with a dead lady from my hometown.

A dead lady who'd apparently (no, obviously!), plucked him somehow from the middle of an engulfing blaze. Ike couldn't remember that. All he could recall now was the annihilating heat. The he'd passed out and awakened seated here, next to Dead Mary. His face was blistered; so were his palms. His lungs ached badly.

Crazy! Totally nuts.

"What year is this?" he finally asked.

"I believe it's 1934," Dead Mary replied. "In a manner of speaking."

" 'A manner of speaking?' What's *that* mean?"

Dead Mary's jaw jutted fractionally. "It's 1934," she said.

Ike nodded. "That's what I thought."

"You still haven't told me why you called the house before, Dwight."

"I needed to know . . . why you gave that photograph to my sister. You said that Del was lost, and there was nothing you could do to help Alice find her. But then you gave her that photograph. How come?"

"Don't use colloquialisms. It's better merely to say: Why?"

"Please, Mrs. Dunham, don't do this! Could you just— tell me?"

Behind Ike, the fire truck—an old-fashioned hook-and-ladder—finally arrived, followed closely by two police vehicles. He could hear men's voices shouting, car doors slamming. Then, a powerful gush of hose water, a loud sizzling, and a tumultuous, roaring hiss. Steam clouds on the breeze. And the oppressive smell of wet ash. "Over here!" somebody yelled. "Direct some o' that over here!" *O-vah he-ah!*

"Mrs. Dunham? . . ." said Ike.

Dead Mary sat up straighter in her bed, carefully smoothing wrinkles from the counterpane that was drawn over her body. Then she half-turned and glowered down at Ike. "I told your sister that her friend Delores—"

"It's Del. Just Del."

"It's Delores—and don't interrupt! Where are your manners?"

"Excuse me."

"Her name, for your information, is Delores Marie Schofield. From Bayonne, New Jersey—originally."

Ike's jaw dropped. Del had always said she was born in the Midwest. Bayonne, New Jersey?

"Shall I proceed, Dwight?"

"Yes. Please."

But before Dead Mary could speak another word, Ike flinched and half-jumped from his seat as two men in flannel shirts, jeans, and thick-soled rubber boots came tramping by, less than five feet away from the chair and the giant bed. They each carried a long-barreled flashlight, the powerful yellow beams bouncing and swiveling ahead of them.

"Looks okay out here," said one of the men.

"But let's just make sure, all right?" said his companion. "One little spark and we could have ourselves another fire. Check over there, Jim." He lifted an arm and pointed directly at Ike.

"Quit fidgeting, Dwight," said Dead Mary. "They can't see us."

"They can't?"

Dead Mary allowed herself a gruff chuckle. "If they could, don't you think they'd have been over here by now?"

The man called Jim shone his light directly into Ike's face, then walked toward him, and then straight through him.

Ike didn't feel a thing.

"Satisfied?" asked Dead Mary.

Weakly, Ike nodded.

"All right, then," she said. "I was telling you about Delores Schofield. Or rather, boy, I was trying to tell you why I'd

118

hoped to dissuade your lovely sister from trying to find that silly girl."

Ike bristled, but kept his mouth closed. Silly girl? Del wasn't silly, Del was . . .

Wonderful.

"Dwight! Are you listening?"

He nodded again, then, realizing that Dead Mary would probably make some crack about his poor manners, he quickly added, "Yes. I'm listening."

"I tried to steer Alice away from this . . . quest, I suppose she'd call it, because personally I did not think Delores Schofield was the kind of person with whom she ought to associate. She's a liar, Dwight. But worse than that, she's a foolish, selfish thing. She got herself into this trouble all on her own. In fact, she was a willing participant in this ridiculous escapade. At first."

"At first?" said Ike.

"She changed her mind. But by then it was too late."

Ike said, "I don't know what you're talking about."

Dead Mary waved a dismissive hand in his direction. "I've always liked your sister, Dwight. She's a most responsible young lady, and I've felt for her. The poor thing has had to put up with a lot, taking care of an ungrateful lout like yourself. Oh don't grimace, Dwight—your face will freeze."

"I'm not grimacing."

"As you wish. But to return to your sister. I like Alice very much and didn't wish to see her burden herself with another heartbreak."

"So now I'm a heartbreak, too?"

"Hush. I won't tolerate aggression."

"Who's aggressive?"

"You are. All the time. But that's not what we're speaking about. Alice is stuck with you, you're her brother. But I didn't see why she had to be stuck with a perfect stranger who'd only bring her further grief."

To keep still, Ike gripped his hands together in his lap and squeezed.

"Nonetheless," Dead Mary went on, "I gathered that Alice wouldn't take my advice, so I gave her the photograph."

"Why?"

"Because I knew that it would, at the proper time, give her some inkling of the situation in which she was getting herself involved."

"And what's that?"

"Oh, I think you both know by now, Dwight. Perhaps not consciously, but you know. Your friend Delores, who's so enamored of magic and who feels so thoroughly . . . estranged . . . from this world, is about to ready to quit it. To go away."

Ike's stomach squeezed out a painful spasm. "Go away . . . to where?"

Raising an arm, Dead Mary pointed past his shoulder across the field, to the place where the tents had all burned down. The sodden ashes were being sifted through by a small army of puzzled men and women. "To where all those orphans went," said Dead Mary, "this night in 1934. *Away.* Far away."

"But she . . . hasn't gone yet?"

Dead Mary leaned back against her pillows, and stared at the sky.

"Mrs. Dunham?"

"No. Not yet."

"Then there's still time to stop her."

"A little. Not much, though."

"It's Jude, isn't it? She's going with him."

"Of course."

Ike leaned forward, planting his elbows on his thighs, putting his grimy, blistered face into his hands.

"Snap out of it, boy! She chose to do this thing."

"But changed her mind! You said it. You said Del changed her mind. Why?"

"I suggest you ask her that yourself," said Dead Mary. "If you get there in time."

Suddenly, Ike was aware that something was . . . different. Had changed. The sky! It was no longer dark, but rather a soft, twilight gray. And the smell of wet ashes had vanished. And no longer were there any raised, anxious voices drifting across the field behind him.

He glanced around, surprised (but not *very* surprised) to discover that the fire truck, the police cars, and the bewildered crowd were no longer there. Neither was there any smoldering trace of the multiple tent fires.

He was staring directly across the open, fallow field at Jude Hayser's farmhouse and barn. In his own time.

Ike jumped to his feet.

"Dwight!"

He felt an insistent tap on his arm. Dead Mary was jabbing him with her long, wrinkled index finger. "I believe you owe me twenty dollars, boy. Let's make it twenty-five. Ten for my information, and fifteen for saving your sorry carcass."

But he broke away, sprinting toward the house.

Behind him, Dead Mary bellowed, "Don't think you can welsh on me, Dwight Fuelle! Don't you think that for even one second."

He tripped and sprawled, and while he was scrambling back onto his feet, he felt positive that, somehow, Dead Mary had been responsible.

He wondered for a moment whether all ghosts were as mercenary as she was. Then he put her out of his mind entirely as he leaped up the soft, almost rotten steps of Jude Hayser's front porch.

26

The same moment that Ike Fuelle raised a fist to pound on the farmhouse door, he changed his mind. Surprise, he thought. *That's* the best way to approach this. Take 'im by surprise.

He was grateful that, for once at least, he'd managed to curb his impulsive behavior.

His hand closed around the doorknob.

No good. Still locked.

Ike racked his brains, trying to figure what to do next. *How* to take Jude Hayser by surprise. Finally, he moved to the end of the porch, slipping past each window as quickly as he could, then climbed over the railing and dropped three feet to an untended flower bed crisp with old leaves, roots, and dead perennials. He sidled several paces to his right and flattened himself against the side of the house.

From where he was standing, he could see the ramshackle barn twenty yards away. Ike briefly considered setting it on fire. Then when Jude came rushing out, he could duck into the house, grab Del, and be gone.

But what if—what if he couldn't *find* Del, or find her quickly enough? Or what if, God forbid, she really wasn't in the house? Then his goose would really be cooked, wouldn't it? He'd end up serving time in a Virginia penitentiary, a convicted arsonist.

Ike scrutinized that train of thought and was positively amazed at himself.

In less than a minute, he'd made two conscious decisions not to behave with his usual recklessness, his typical imprudence.

Man, what was *happening*?

He wasn't acting like himself at *all* today.

Good, he thought. I like this me better. The new me.

Okay, but new Ike or old, he still had to find some way to get inside the farmhouse. Think. Think, Fuelle, he urged himself. *Think!*

He pulled at his hair and shifted his feet—*think!*—and softly tapped the heal of a sneaker against a ground-level windowpane.

So much for thought.

Now just pray, he told himself.

Pray the cellar window is unlocked.

Kneeling down beside it, he clenched a fist and batted gently at the frame. Chips and pebbles of desiccated putty sprinkled Ike's knuckles. The four small panes were opaqued with whitewash from inside. He pushed harder.

The window shifted inward a mere quarter-inch.

He pushed again, now with the heels of both hands, and felt resistance. At last there was a soft crunching sound, and the hinged window swung fully in.

Glancing behind him to make sure that Jude Hayser wasn't sneaking around the corner of the house, Ike held up the window with his palm, like a waiter carrying a tray of drinks, while he scooted around, stuck his legs through first, then dropped carefully into the dark, musty basement.

He cursed to himself when the window slammed closed after him.

His sneakers sank into the thick, powdery dirt floor of the cellar.

He assumed there'd be stairs leading up into the house, but so far his eyes hadn't adapted sufficiently to the gloom for him to see anything. Stretching out an arm, Ike started forward, walking bent from the waist because of the low ceiling—and taking it very slowly. With practically every step, he peeled away another cobweb.

It was like trudging on a beach, and in a matter of seconds, his sneakers were full of dirt. He bumped against something solid and recoiled. Tentatively, Ike's fingers reached out and touched a massive, ancient coal furnace.

He skirted it and moved on, sneakers, knees, or hips occasionally bumping against something else: an empty metal toolbox, the legs of a workbench, a rusty old bicycle with flat tires that leaned precariously against its kickstand. He almost knocked that over and had to grab the bike as it teetered. When he blindly readjusted the kickstand, there was a loud *skeerk!* that stopped his heart for a second and made his hair stand on end.

He froze, anticipating discovery.

But nobody came.

By this time, his vision had adjusted to the darkness, and Ike now had a rough idea of the cellar's full size and dimensions. It ran the entire length and width of the farmhouse. And now, as he bumped against a shoulder-height plank wall, he realized why he hadn't seen any stairs, the coal bin, here, had blocked his view.

Quickly he went around it, crunching through powder till he came to the foot of the stairs. Looking up, he saw a door outlined in a pale light that leaked through from its opposite side.

What if *that's* locked? he thought.

Well, you won't know till you try it.

He crept up silently toward the door, taking each tread with care, testing it before he put down his full weight. But when Ike was three steps from the top, he flinched, pinning his elbows tightly to his ribs. He'd heard a noise.

It sounded—possibly—like somebody walking around.

But he'd come this far, so . . .

He climbed the last several steps, then paused with his head cocked and an ear pressed against the cool surface of the door. When a minute passed and Ike hadn't heard another sound, his hand went, trembling, to the knob.

Easing the door open a crack, he peered into a large, empty kitchen. The window shades—brittle, yellowed, and mended, long ago, with tape—were drawn past the sills, giving the room a sepulchral feel. There was a Formica-topped table with metal legs and, set around it, three cane-bottomed chairs, each likely to collapse the moment anyone sat down. Also, a white and badly chipped enameled oven from long-bygone days and a refrigerator from the same era, a dry sink, a wet sink, and a black Baltimore stove fitted snugly into a brick chimney.

The black-and-white linoleum was cracked, warped, and filthy. Dust clumps the size of cantaloupes were everywhere—climbing the table legs, wadding the corners, and hugging the square floor tiles like soft gray chessmen. On the wall hung a calendar two years out of date.

There wasn't a plate, dish, bowl, cup, or drinking glass evident. Nobody had eaten anything in *this* kitchen lately. And possibly not for quite some time.

Holding his breath and hearing his heart boom in his ears, Ike, using just his fingertips, pushed the door open wide enough for him to squeeze through.

But now that he was inside the house—what?

Move.

Investigate.

Find her, he told himself.

Find Del.

An archway to his left, led, Ike realized, to the main hall he'd seen when he peered through the front door. He took a step toward the archway, then stopped.

A weapon, he thought.

And what better place to find one than in a kitchen? He glanced around, spotting a pair of drawers in the counter between the stove and the wet sink. He pulled out the first drawer, but discovered only a tangle of rubber bands, a box of matches, and a bottle of glue. The second drawer, though, had cutlery in it, and Ike helped himself to a long carving knife with a heavy, gnarled grip. As soon as he held it, he felt better.

Although he was not at all sure that he would ever be able to *stab* anybody.

125

Worry about that, he thought, when the time comes.

Then, Please, he thought, don't let the time come.

As he turned away from the drawers, he felt a sudden draft of cool air blow across his face. Spinning around, he faced the kitchen door—a back door—and found it standing ajar.

Through the opening he glimpsed Jude Hayser seated on a small iron bench out in the yard. With his palms capped on his knees, he was leaning forward, staring at his father's grave mound. Evening was coming on fast—Jude was nearly a silhouette.

Carefully, Ike tiptoed over and closed the door. Then he thumbed the lock down.

With a tight, satisfied grin, he hurried through the kitchen and down the central hall. Bracing a hand on the newel post, he vaulted up the staircase—taking it two, three stairs at a time.

Heading for the attic.

Of course.

27

Over the last couple of years, in his capacity as a guitarist in the Jersey midlands music scene (such as it was), Bo Cudhy had been mistaken several times for a Straight Edger. But no way! Personally, he didn't have much sympathy or patience with kids who played, or paid for, that kind of punk. Because they all seemed so priggishly smug and intolerant. Several months earlier, he'd been at a concert in Hoboken and had seen a pack of Straight Edgers attack and beat up a guy just for toking on a joint. Those people flat-out made him sick, and he bristled whenever somebody figured him for one. And the only reason he was so identified—misidentified—was because, like Straight Edgers, he didn't drink, dope, or smoke. His abstinence from that stuff, however, had nothing to do with morals or politics. He just didn't do that stuff, period. It was a personal decision, and if somebody else wanted to do it, well, that was their business. Bo never passed judgment.

Well, almost never.

Right now, almost choking to death on Greg Odet's foul cigar smoke, he had to admit that he thought the guy was an A-number-one idiot. How could he *stand* that stench? For sure, Bo couldn't. Cigarette smoke was bad enough, but *cigar* smoke? Deadly. Bo felt assaulted by the drifting blue haze, his eyes burned and his throat was raw from breathing it in, and his temples—man, his temples were crashing like cymbals. Headache City.

Bo didn't know how much longer he could take it. Silently, he urged Alice and Fletch to hurry it up, hurry up with the questions, already, and let's get the heck outta here!

Trying not to draw attention to himself by fanning away

smoke, Bo declined to take a seat when they all trudged into Odet's home fifteen minutes earlier. (The fat realtor had his long black cigar lit when he opened the front door to let them in.)

Alice and Fletch sat down together on a small sofa facing Odet, who ensconced himself in a huge leather wing chair. Bo loitered in the background, and Ramona, bless her, had stayed by his side.

As Fletch prodded Odet with questions about Del, and as Odet, puffing away, deliberately seemed to avoid answering any of them directly, Bo had just waved a hand in front of his face, or turned his back on the conversation and idly strolled around the formal parlor.

Greg Odet lived in a pretty cool house, in Bo's opinion, But it was the kind of place that made him nervous, too, he was afraid that he'd bump into one of the many small mahogany tables and knock over a vase, or a decorative plate, or a family photograph in a pewter frame, or some puny porcelain knickknack that probably cost a thousand bucks. So when he moved about the room, he moved carefully, and Ramona followed him with sympathetic eyes.

Right away, she'd picked up on his smoke aversion, though he hadn't said a word about it or signaled her in the least.

Now he stood with his hands clasped behind him, staring up at a huge oil painting that hung over the fireplace mantel.

It was a picture of General Robert E. Lee astride his horse. The oval plate affixed to the bottom of the ornate frame read, "Lee and Traveller."

When Bo first saw it hanging there, he scrutinized it for a secret image, thinking that maybe the painting was an expensive version of those woozy hidden-picture things you saw for sale at big shopping malls. He searched every inch of the painting, looking for a second guy, the guy named Traveller. After a while, though, he realized that Traveller was the horse. Just the horse.

A fresh cloud of acrid smoke came wafting past his head

now, and he had to squeeze his nose or else he'd be coughing in three more seconds.

Ramona came and dropped her hand on his shoulder. Bo turned and smiled at her. She moved her eyes sidelong, indicating Fletch, Alice, and Greg Odet, then raised her eyes quizzically.

Bo shrugged.

He didn't know why this was taking so long, either.

Very weird.

Fletch answered the phone when Greg Odet called the motel—everyone else had been too rattled by the burning photograph. Yes, Odet said, he'd spotted one of the flyers and thought he might have some information about the missing girl. But when Fletch asked him where he'd seen her, Odet turned cagey. That's the word Fletch used himself after he hung up, "cagey."

Odet refused to tell Fletch anything more over the telephone, and insisted that he come see him at his home on Monument Avenue. Fletch agreed—though Bo could tell that he was annoyed about it.

They left a note for Ike in both rooms before they left the motel.

Ramona and Bo drove over in Ramona's car, Fletch and Alice followed in the van.

Odet lived not quite fifteen minutes' drive from the motel, in a large brick house on a swank street that was divided in the middle by a broad parklike median.

At every cross street on Monument Avenue stood a towering statue of a different Civil War general. The only one that Bo had ever heard of was Lee.

He figured that was because in New Jersey they taught the Union generals in high school, and skimped on the Confederate ones. Which sort of made sense.

Greg Odet was surprised to discover four people standing on his front steps, he was expecting just Fletch. But he quickly smoothed out his frown, smiled brightly around his smoking cigar, and graciously invited them all inside.

But when he got a good look at Ramona, his forehead bunched thickly again. "We've met, I believe," Odet said, and Ramona nodded. "At the Hayser farm!" Odet added, his memory fully jogged. Then, abruptly, his eyes narrowed and he grew very suspicious—even cagier than he'd been on the phone.

For the past fifteen minutes, Fletch had been trying to get a few simple answers from him—where had he seen Del? When?—but Odet kept turning things around, wanting to know who Del was, exactly, and why they were looking for her.

Though chagrined, Fletch played it cool, remained affable. Alice, though, was getting antsier by the second.

Right now, as Bo was finally tiring of staring at General Lee and Traveller, Alice blurted, "Mr. Odet, is there something I'm missing here? Why won't you just tell us what we want to know? You're stalling!"

"Miss Fuelle,"—he pronounced the name *few-ell*—"if you think I'm stalling, well then, I apologize. I was just trying to make conversation."

"We're not interested in conversation, Mr. Odet," she snapped. "We're interested in finding our friend."

"Yes, of course," he replied smoothly, blowing another jet of blue smoke. "Of course. But you understand, I'm merely trying to ascertain what's going on here." He leaned forward, plucked the cigar from his mouth, and scanned Alice's face. With an unpleasant smile, he said, "I'm wondering if a crime has been committed."

"I don't see how that's any of your business," said Fletch.

"But if I'm to become involved—"

"All we want to know is where you've seen her," said Alice. "Just tell us where, for crying out loud!"

"Please calm down," said Odet. "As I say, if a crime has been committed, a kidnaping perhaps—"

"Who said anything about kidnapping?" cried Alice.

Greg Odet sat back in his wing chair. He slid the cigar

between his pursed lips, his cheeks moving in and out like bellows. A cloud of smoke erupted around his head.

"Look," said Alice, "do you want money? Is that it? Are you fishing for some reward?"

Narrowing his eyes, Greg Odet looked amused—then his expression swiftly turned disagreeable. "That was uncalled for," he said.

There was a long, awkward pause—broken finally by a sudden explosion of racking coughs.

" 'Scuse me," said Bo, heading quickly across the parlor (nearly tripping on the Persian rug) and out into the foyer. Still coughing, he pulled open the inside door, stepped across the vestibule, pulled open the outside door, and escaped into the fresh air.

Ramona came out two seconds behind him and gently patted his back while he stood bent over with his hands flat on his thighs, wheezing.

"You okay? Bo?"

"Yeah, I'll be fine." He straightened up and knuckled tears from the corners of his eyes. "Man, though, do I hate that guy's cigars."

"I just hate the guy."

Bo glanced up and met her look. Her expression was stony, but a little distant, too—thoughtful. "What?" he said.

"He saw her at Jude's farm," said Ramona.

"You think?"

"I *know*. It *has* to be that."

"So why doesn't he just say so?"

"That's what I was trying to figure out. But I only got it when he mentioned a crime being committed—when he brought up kidnaping. That creep!" She smiled bitterly, then put her arm around Bo's shoulders and walked with him down the brick steps to the pavement.

The sky had grown dark while they'd been inside.

"Maybe I'm dense, Ramona, but . . . what're you saying?"

"You know why he keeps pumping us? He *hopes* that Del's been kidnaped. And he wants Jude to be the bad guy."

"He probably is."

"He probably is, you're right. But Greg Odet doesn't care a fig about Del. In fact, I'll bet you he's even hoping that she's . . . well, never mind."

Bo rubbed his jaw, nodding. "I'm beginning to see the light. If Jude Hayser snatched Del, then he's a criminal. Which'll make it easier for Cigar Man to get the property and sell it. Is that what you're thinking?"

"Yes," said Ramona. "That's it."

"We couldn't get the cops to go poke around that farm, but Odet could, probably. So he's trying to make Fletch say it—say that there's been a kidnapping. Then Odet picks up the phone . . ."

"Exactly."

Bo thought for a few seconds. "So maybe we should go and tell Fletch that's what he ought to say. I mean . . . whatever we could do to get Del back—shouldn't we try it?"

Ramona looked at him. "You're probably right."

"That's nice to hear for a change. Hardly anybody ever tells me that."

She laughed, and her eyes glistened with affection. "I like you, Cudhy—for a Yankee you're not half-bad."

"Thank you, ma'am. But I thought you were a Yankee yourself."

"Half and half," said Ramona. Then, after a pause, "So, do you want to go back inside and have a little conference with Fletch and Alice?"

"Wild horses couldn't get me back in there."

"Want just me to go, then?"

For sure Bo didn't, not when he had Ramona all to himself for awhile. He gave a half-shrug, and finally said, "If they're not out in ten minutes, *then* we'll decide—okay?"

"Okay."

Bo took Ramona by the hand and led her across the pavement to her Mirage, parked at the curb four cars in front of Alice's van. She perched on the hood, and he stood in front of her.

For a couple of minutes, they just looked at each other.

"I know it sounds terrible," Bo said, then trailed off.

"What sounds terrible?"

"No, never mind."

"Tell me."

He bit down on his underlip, then dragged his front teeth over it till it popped free. "I mean . . . I shouldn't be thinking about anything else but finding Del, except . . ."

Ramona lifted an eyebrow.

"Except," he continued, "I keep thinking about . . . how much I'm gonna hate to go home when this is all done. Whether it's tonight, which I guess seems pretty unlikely now, or . . . whenever. I'll miss you."

"Thank you, Bo."

"And?"

She laughed. "I'll miss you, too. But this isn't exactly Australia. You could come back. From time to time."

He brightened. "Yeah! Or you could come up to Jersey. Yeah?"

"Sure."

"You, um, like living here?"

"You already asked me that once. And yeah, I like it enough."

"Enough that you wouldn't, you know, consider moving?"

"To where, New Jersey?"

"Well . . ."

"I still have two more years of college."

"Right," said Bo, "right."

"How about yourself? You think you could move down here?"

"Do you have to pass a test first?"

"A test?"

"I mean, if you gotta name five Confederate generals, I'm sunk."

"No test. No official one, at least."

"Well, that's a relief." Bo took several steps backward, then looked up and down the street. "Man, it's quiet here. Quiet city, huh?"

"In neighborhoods like this—absolutely. But it can get pretty noisy in other ones. Last year, Richmond had more murders than any city in the country except New Orleans."

"Geez," said Bo. "You'd never know it."

"On a rich, comfortable street like Monument Avenue, no, you wouldn't. You never would. But I could show you some places . . ."

"Yeah? *Would* you?" He blushed suddenly. "No, that came out wrong. What I mean is—would you show me around? *All* around? If I asked you to?"

"Sure. My pleasure."

Bo figured it was now or never and worth the risk. He leaned over, put his face just inches from Ramona, smiled, and kissed her.

She kissed him back.

Just as they were about to try that again, the neighborhood's eerie quiet was shattered by a screech of tires and a siren's wail.

A red TransAm swung around the corner doing seventy, taking it on two tires. The car slammed down, bounced, veered, straightened, then raced west along Monument Avenue. Bo caught just a glimpse of the passengers: two or three teenaged boys, all of them terrified. The driver was hunched over the wheel.

"Man, what the heck is—"

A police car rounded the same corner, at the same dangerous speed.

One of its tires blew out.

Instinctively, Bo grabbed Ramona and yanked her away from the Mirage. While his back was turned, he heard the solid, sickening crash of metal against metal—metal shearing metal—followed by a thunderous explosion of glass.

The patrol car had collided with Alice's parked van, and propelled it—now a crumpled hulk—halfway across the sidewalk.

As Bo raced toward it, he could see a uniformed policeman kick open the driver's door and slide out from under the wheel of the patrol car.

"Is this your vehicle?" the cop asked, then touched a hand to his forehead, it came away wet with blood. Nasty gash there, two inches long. "I asked you, is this your vehicle."

"No, sir," said Bo.

Instantly, the cop—a sandy-haired guy who looked like he'd just graduated high school last spring—gripped Bo by the wrist. "I need your car. This is police business!"

"I don't have a car," said Bo.

"I do!" Ramona stepped forward, pulling a ring of keys from her pocket. The cop snatched it from her hand.

"Which?" he said.

"The Mirage," she answered, pointing.

Without another word, the cop sprinted up the street, flung open the driver's door, jumped in, started the ignition, pulled out, then floored it.

With their mouths hanging open, Bo and Ramona watched him disappear.

Up and down both sides of the street, people came pouring out of their expensive brick houses and were staring in bafflement at the collision scene.

Bo saw Alice frozen in shock on the top step of Greg Odet's house. Fletch was coming down the steps, his expression a combination of disbelief, rage, and (if Bo wasn't mistaken) despair.

"Do you believe this mess?" said Bo.

Fletch just shook his head. Then, "We're up the creek now, you know that?"

With a frown, Bo said, "It'll be okay. Alice has insurance."

"That's not it! How are we supposed to get out to Hayser's farm?"

"What?"

Fletch glared at him. "Odet just told us. That's where he saw Del! *That's where she is!*"

Squeezing his forehead, Bo Cudhy half-turned and looked behind him at the mangled wreckage of Alice's van.

And God only knew where Ramona's car was at the moment. Or when they'd get it back.

28

Del Schofield was dead.

As Ike had raced through the farmhouse—trampling up the first staircase, then down a short passageway, then up more stairs—he kept mumbling to himself, Be there, Del, be there, be in the attic. . . .

And she was, looking emaciated, lying on a stained gray mattress no thicker than a paperback novel. Wearing the same Godzilla T-shirt that she'd had on the day Ike had first seen her. That T-shirt, soiled and wrinkled, was slightly rucked up around her flat belly. T-shirt, black jeans. Barefoot. . . .

Del was there, but her face was ghastly white—she was dead. Her glassy eyes stared fixedly at the large canvas tent staked to the plank floor several feet away.

Her hands and feet were bound, cinched tightly, with heavy clothesline.

And she was dead.

Ike's knife clattered to the floor.

He shut his eyes, staggered, then heard a loud, quavering, desolate moan came from his throat. The sound kept on, and kept on, till it filled the whole attic.

"Ike?"

He froze, eyes still closed tight.

"Ike? Oh my God, it's you! *Ike!*"

Then his eyes were open, wide open, and he was staring across the room, seeing blearily. Del had shifted position, had raised herself onto an elbow and was gazing back at him with stunned incredulity.

Ike's relief was so violent that his head felt as though it might blow off his neck, a wave of red-stained blackness

136

washed through his vision. Then—unaccountably, giddily, almost scarily—he laughed.

When he took a step toward Del, he almost crashed to the floor, his legs were so wobbly, that rubbery.

The laughter died in his chest. Looking at Del now, seeing her look back at him with a dazed, pleading expression, Ike's euphoria was followed by a cold fury.

He wanted to kill somebody.

And he knew exactly who that somebody was.

"Ike? . . ."

"I'm here," he said. "For real."

He dropped onto one knee and reached a hand cautiously toward her. When he touched Del's cool cheek, she turned her face and pressed her mouth against his palm.

And then his head *did* blow off his neck.

Or felt as though it did.

He cupped his other hand around the back of Del's head, drawing her toward him; she lay against his chest for a long, long moment, her sobs and shudders passing into Ike like bullets. He drew a stabilizing breath and glared rigidly past her, seeing cardboard boxes heaped with old clothes and books and dusty curtains, a few broken chairs, a pair of end tables furry with dust, a jumble of extension cords, a torn lampshade, a crate heaped with chipped dishes. Propped against that was Del's book of magic.

"I'm gonna get you out of here," he said, and gripped Del's hands, turned them gently, searching for the knot in the clothesline. He found it, started working it free.

"Ike? . . ."

"Don't talk, okay? Let me just . . ."

"You got a candy bar, or something?"

That stopped him.

He glanced into her gaunt face. "What?"

"I'm starving! I haven't eaten anything in I don't know how long!"

"What? Why?"

"I'll tell you about it later. But . . . you really don't have anything?"

"To eat? Jeez, no. I'm sor—"

"It's all right. Just . . . get me out of this place!"

"But why was that creep starving you?"

"I'll tell you later, okay?"

His hands fumbled with the knot, he broke a thumbnail and he cursed.

"Take your time, take your time. . . ."

Ike hissed, "We don't *have* time!"

"You got that right," said Jude Hayser, and when Ike pivoted around to look, he caught just a glimpse of something curved and black moving toward him. Then his head filled completely with a glossy red light that seemed almost liquid.

29

Slowly, woozily, Ike regained consciousness, swimming up through the dark red, then pink, then pink-tinged, then milk-white medium surrounding him. When he opened his eyes, the first thing he saw was Jude Hayser's face, fractured into a thousand shivering pieces. The pieces coalesced into a whole. Ike felt a pain in his skull, just above his left ear, start to throb.

He lurched forward, but toppled onto his side.

His arms were twisted behind him, his hands crossed and his wrists bound together. So were his legs, at the ankles and around his thighs. With heavy-duty orange extension cords.

Jude's face loomed, large and hostile.

Ike's head snapped to one side as Jude slapped him.

Jude looked at his open palm, leaned back on his haunches, leaned forward again, and slapped Ike again.

Ike felt his bottom lip split open, and he tasted blood, salt, and copper.

He tried to spit at Jude, but his mouth was too dry.

"Where are all your friends?" Jude asked.

Ike glared, then smiled slowly. "Don't worry, they'll be along."

"Oh, yes?" Jude smiled back. "Maybe so, maybe not. Either way, it doesn't matter. Del and I won't be here very much longer." He stood up, looked over at Del still lying on the mattress, then walked to the medallion window and peered through the round, filthy pane.

Outside, it was night, full dark.

"Our two-week fast is up tonight," he said, almost to himself. He grinned at Del. "We can leave any time we like now." Turning his head, he stared intently at the big wall tent.

139

Ike thought, Two weeks? Del hasn't eaten anything for two weeks? Not since . . .

Not since she told Bo and Fletch that she was staying in Richmond and then vanished.

She's been starving here in this crummy attic for *two weeks?*

"You're crazy!" he blurted. "You are absolutely, totally—"

"Ike," cried Del, "please don't! Don't get him angry—please!"

Too late. Jude Hayser's eyes blazed and his hand closed around the grip of his revolver, which he still wore stuck into his waistband. "I only *hit* you with this before. I could just as well shoot you with it." He yanked it free and brandished it. "You want that, Jersey boy? *Want that?*"

Gumming his lips, praying that he looked sufficiently cowed, Ike shook his head. "But I want—"

"What do you want? *What?*"

This guy, thought Ike, is flipping out, losing it.

Get him calm.

Calm 'im down.

Or else . . . we're sunk. Me and Del. Del and me.

"Look," said Ike, squirming around on the floor a little, propping his back against an attic wall, he could feel the cool night air blowing softly through chinks. "Look, I just want to . . . to know what you're doing. What's going on."

"It doesn't concern you."

"Jude!" Even raised, calling out, Del's voice sounded weak, tremulous. "He's an orphan, too. Ike's like us."

"Liar!"

"No," said Del, "it's true."

Jude narrowed his eyes and cocked his head. Then he moved slowly across the attic floor, keeping his gaze fixed on Ike, studying him. "I don't believe her," he said.

"I don't really care," said Ike.

Jude stuck his revolver back into his waistband. Then he bent his knees and crouched, peering at Ike so baldly, so penetratingly that Ike wanted to avert his eyes. But he didn't;

140

for some reason he knew it was important to hold Jude's gaze.

Finally, Jude Hayser nodded, allowed himself a fleeting smile, and stood up to his full height again.

"I see it, yes. In your eyes. The anger."

"You're damn straight there's anger," Ike shot back.

"No, no, no—not just ordinary anger. *Orphan's* anger."

Ike swallowed and let his eyes drift, he met Del's gaze. And saw her shake her head almost imperceptibly.

Her expression and her gesture combined told him: Jude's stone-crazy, but humor him. Just humor him.

"Yes," said Jude now, "I see it! You have it, Jersey boy. The anger. The pain." He shook his head. "Sorry, though. There's only one tent. Just room for two."

"I understand," said Ike. "I understand."

Humor him. String him along.

"But . . . seeing as how I'm . . . like you and Del, maybe you could tell me what you're doing. What I'm . . . missing."

Jude said, "We're going to the other place, the Orphans' World. We're going home to our true family. Our own kind."

Ike said, "How?"

"The tent, of course. It's the gate. The doorway!" Jude strode back across the floor, to the tent. He grabbed one of the flaps in a fist. "This is our symbol, isn't it? The tent. Transitory, lacking all comfort—the cruelest shelter in a hostile world. The Orphan's tent. But thanks to Thomas Dunbar Lawrence, it's a symbol of passage—and the *method,* too. *Our* method of passage! To a better place, a world of our own."

As crazy as a bedbug, Ike thought. But he said, "Thomas Dunbar Lawrence?"

"The Orphan Thomas!"

"Yes. But . . ."

"Orphaned at the age of seven. Mistreated in one public orphanage after another, 'adopted' by men and women who worked him cruelly for their own financial gain. A nobody. A thing. A person-thing. Who cared about his suffering? Not

141

a living soul! He was a boy of genius and talent, although his brilliance was never recognized."

"What kind of talent?" said Ike.

"He possessed a special kind of knowledge. Instinctual knowledge. Magic was in him. He *perceived*."

"I don't—"

"He knew there were other worlds, empty worlds, fresh and green and beautiful worlds separated from this one by just a breath, the merest breath. And he was determined to find a way to get *through*. And at last, he found it."

"How do you know all this stuff?"

With a triumphant leer, Jude Hayser nodded at the tent. "When the Orphan Thomas was ready, he let the word go out—a rumor dropped at one orphanage spread to another, and to another, and another, and then spread to the orphan trains—a call to meet. And those who had the wisdom to understand, they fled their bondage and their misery and found their way . . . here. To this farm. My great-grandfather's farm. Sixty years ago.

"Thomas Dunbar Lawrence paid my great-grandfather three hundred dollars for the use of his field. And for two full weeks, the Orphan Thomas instructed his fellow orphans about the Migration. And as they learned of the new world that was to be theirs, only theirs, they fasted—cleansing themselves entirely of the pollution of this world."

Jude came and stood over Ike.

"And my grandfather, who was just a boy of fourteen at the time, listened every day. And heard everything. About the magic, about the other world—about how a tentmaker's apprentice had constructed gateways to paradise out of cheap white canvas.

"And on the last night, on Migration Night, the Orphan Thomas announced that all of the tents should be doused with gasoline—"

Ike's eyes snapped wide open, and without thinking he gave a decisive, corroborative nod. Jude looked startled.

"You know about this?" he asked.

"It was, um—on television. I saw something about it."

Suspiciously, Jude stared at him for a long moment, then nodded. "Yes."

"But why burn the tents?"

"So that nobody could follow, of course! This new world would be populated by only those orphans who first heard the call, who believed in the magic of the Orphan Thomas—and took the leap of faith. All the tents would be burned. And Thomas Dunbar Lawrence would burn them all."

"All of them didn't get burned, though," said Ike. And he gestured with his head toward the tent behind Jude.

"No. One tent was saved. *His* tent. And do you know why?"

Ike said, "Your grandfather pulled it down and saved it."

Jude's mouth dropped open.

Ike said, "Good guess, huh?" And he remembered that feral farm boy who'd shoved him away from the tent, who beat out the sparks with an old army blanket. Jude's grandfather. Of course.

"And this tent stayed bundled up in my attic for decades. When my grandfather was alive, he'd tell me all about those two weeks in 1934 when the orphans lived on our land."

"A family story," said Ike.

"Exactly. A family story."

"And you never tried to . . . use it?"

Jude laughed. "Of course! What boy wouldn't? But it was hopeless. I wasn't an orphan, was I? Not then. And not for a long time. Not till recently. And besides," he added, "it was two-by-two."

"Two-by-two?"

"Thomas Dunbar Lawrence insisted that each tent be used by one male and one female. And two-by-two, the orphans would step back through the tent flaps into their Garden of Eden." Jude glanced again toward Del. "So now you understand her . . . involvement."

Ike thrust out his chin. "But she doesn't *want* to go with you! She doesn't want to take any 'leap of faith'!"

"She did! When we first met and I told her about the Migration, about the tent in my attic, about the magic, she agreed to come. To come with me."

"When you told me about it," Del cried, "you never mentioned . . . never coming back!"

Jude pivoted around and glared at her. "I heard your songs, girl—I heard them! You're not part of this world, you've never felt at home here—never. Admit it!"

"Jude, please . . ."

"I've heard your songs! And I heard you sing them! In our new world there won't be any loneliness! There won't be any families to fall apart and leave you all by yourself! There will be just one family—all of us who know. Who know how it *feels* to be abandoned . . . to lose everything!"

"How do you know," said Ike, "*what* this place is gonna be like?"

"I trust in the Orphan Thomas!"

He shouted with such vehemence that both Del and Ike were shocked into silence. They watched him stand there, breathing heavily, then he prowled to the back of the attic and dragged a carton stuffed with old clothing into the center of the room. He plucked out a faded plaid shirt, held it dangling in his hand. Then he fetched a lighter from his pocket, got a flame, and lit the tail of the shirt.

"Time to go," he said. He flung away the burning shirt; it landed in a flickering heap in the corner. A flame rose up and nibbled at the wall. He looked at Ike and shook his head. "I'm sorry," he said. "But I can't let you leave, can I?"

"You're not—!"

"I said I was sorry." He pulled out a pair of frayed pants, lit one of the legs, and hurled them away. The pants fell against a cardboard box full of dishes, the cardboard glimmered into small flames.

He lit another shirt and tossed it onto Del's book of magic spells. The pages caught, then flared up.

Ike squirmed and twisted, pulled at his bonds. Nothing

144

gave. "Why do you want to go there, Jude? Why? You weren't some abandoned orphan, for God's sake!"

"This land—that's been in my family for two hundred years—it's depleted, farmed out, dead! And the vultures keep swarming around me. They're going to grab it and build houses, and there's nothing I can do about it! What do I care about their money? Money is nothing to me! If I have to leave this land, I want to leave this world! And I will!"

Grimly, he lit a woman's dress and tossed it away into a carton brimming with gingham window curtains.

Flames whooshed up, licked the ceiling, and began to spread across it.

As Ike watched in horror, Jude Hayser strode across the floor. He grabbed Del roughly by an arm, and dragged her, struggling, toward the tent.

Already the attic was filled with dense black smoke, and flames were racing across the floorboards, crawling along the rafters. Another box of clothing erupted into yellow fire.

"Don't leave me here!" Ike screamed.

Jude gave him a final glance. "Sorry, Jersey boy."

He pulled Del inside the wall tent, and the flaps fell together behind them.

"Ike!" Del shouted. "Ike!"

Her voice, suddenly, seemed very far away.

Then it was gone.

And once again, Ike Fuelle was swallowed up in a conflagration.

Only this time, Mary Dunham failed to appear.

30

As soon as they turned onto the access road, they spotted the flames. And when they came around a curve, moments later, they saw it was the Hayser house burning. Roof engulfed, the orange fire leapt raggedly upward.

"I'm not surprised," groused Greg Odet. "That old place is a tinderbox."

"Just drive," said Fletch, from behind him, and gave him a sharp nudge to the shoulder. "And speed it up."

They'd driven out from Richmond in Odet's Dodge Ram—they couldn't all fit into his Audi.

Odet was not at all gracious about serving as their chauffeur.

Nor had Fletch been at all gracious in dragooning him.

Odet had muttered something about kidnapping.

Fletch, in return, had muttered something about a busted nose.

The Ram sped, jouncing over the hole-filled road. Bo was bounced violently from his seat. His head cracked against the interior light.

"You okay?" said Ramona.

"Great. Great." He rubbed his skull and bounced again—then was pitched forward against the back of the front passenger seat when Odet abruptly jammed on the brakes.

The moment the minivan came to a screeching halt, Alice Fuelle levered open her door—she was riding up front, next to Odet—and tumbled out. She pushed through the fence gate and ran toward the front porch. At the foot of the steps, she halted, clapping a hand to her mouth.

Her head tipped far back and she stared up at the house. To the attic. The medallion window there suddenly burst from the heat; glass shards wheeled and tumbled toward Alice.

Fletch snatched her by the arm and jerked her backward. He pressed her head down, shielded her body with his, and the broken glass slammed down, some bouncing off Fletch's shoulders and back, a few pieces slicing through his shirt, bloodying him.

He ran Alice back across the yard, pushed her through the gate.

"What are you doing?" she screamed. "Del's in there!"

"Let's think a second! Okay?"

Alice opened her mouth to protest, then paused and shrugged in a gesture of helplessness.

Fletch squeezed her elbow, then turned to Greg Odet, who'd climbed out of the Ram and was watching them from across the hood.

"You got a cellular phone in there?" said Fletch.

"Of course," Odet replied. Smugly.

"Then use it. Now! Call the fire department! Call the cops!"

"With pleasure," said Odet, a nasty smirk bending up one corner of his mouth. While he pulled open the driver's door and leaned back into the minivan, Fletch gestured impatiently to Bo and Ramona.

"I'm going in," he told them. "But I think you guys should wait out here. You, too, Alice."

"Forget it," she said.

"Yeah," Bo agreed. "Forget it. So let's not argue, okay? Let's just get in there and get out."

"All right, all right," said Fletch. "But we do it this way. It looks like the fire's still mostly in the attic. When we go in? I'm going straight up there. You three take the first floor and the second. And if the smoke gets too thick, you turn around and get the heck right outta—"

Alice said, "Fletch? Do you want to synchronize watches, too? Skip the plans, all right? Like Bo says, let's just get in there and get out!"

He looked at her and raised his eyebrows. Then he pressed his lips together, nodded, and sharply inclined his head toward the house. "Just be careful," he said.

They raced across the yard and vaulted onto the porch.

Bo threw himself against the door, just the way he'd seen it done a million times before in cop movies—and bounced right off. Then he raised a foot and kicked the door knob with his heel. His sneaker slid sideways and broke the door glass.

"Why don't you reach in now," said Ramona, "and just *open* it. But don't cut yourself."

Bo gave her a quick, wry glance, slipped his arm through the jagged pane, felt around, found the lock, and turned it.

The center hall was curtained with black smoke.

"Check every room," said Fletch, already on the staircase. "And don't forget about Hayser. Keep an eye out for him!"

He started up, with Alice following behind.

At the second floor, Fletch pointed with his thumb—for her to start with that door—but she just pushed him forward. "I'm going to the attic with you. That's where she is, and we both know it!"

"Alice!"

"This isn't the time or place to tell you how much I hate macho men. Move it, Fletcher!"

He shut up and ran forward.

The attic staircase was burning, the wallpaper peeling off in fiery curls. Underfoot, the rubber tread-guards had turned gooey.

The downdraft, the heat, and the foaming black smoke made the climb to the attic feel like a hundred miles. It was a confused, almost impossible ascent. Fletch reached a hand back and panicked when he didn't touch Alice. "Keep going!" he heard her shout behind him, then she barked a cough.

At last, he stumbled onto the attic floor.

"Del!" he shouted. "Del!"

Directly in front of him stood the wall tent, the canvas

burning in a dozen places, fire racing along its still-taut guy-lines.

Snatching at one of the tent flaps, Fletch yanked it open. The tent was empty.

In back of him, lost somewhere in the flames and the smoke, Alice called Del's name again.

Then Fletch heard her cry, "My God!"

He spun around. "You found her?" He waved his hands desperately in front of his face, trying to clear his way to see . . . something. Anything. "Alice? You found her?"

"It's Ike!"

Fletch's first thought was that the smoke had gotten to her, that Alice had become dangerously confused, overwhelmed by the hectic, swirling conflagration. But then he heard Ike's voice.

Ike's voice! Yelling, "The tent—get the tent!"

Then Alice's voice: "I need help! Fletch! He's tied up!"

Ike's voice: "The tent! Save the tent!"

After a moment's hesitation, Fletch dropped to the attic floor, where the smoke was less dense and roiling. He crawled forward, heat scorching his chest, splinters snagging on his shirtfront.

He touched something, something that moved.

It was Alice on her knees, bent over her brother.

She was struggling to untie several extension cords that were lashed around Ike's legs and wrists.

"No," said Fletch, "let's just carry him out of here. No time for that."

"You have to take the tent," said Ike weakly. "She's in the tent."

"No," said Fletch, "I looked."

"You don't understand," said Ike, then he coughed and struggled when Fletch tried scooping him up into his arms. "That tent's the only way we can get her back! Don't let it burn!"

"It's already burning. Damn it, Ike—quit fighting me!"

"The tent!" said Ike. "You have to—"

"Sorry, pal," said Fletch after he'd driven his fist against Ike's jaw and knocked him unconscious. Then he lifted Ike into his arms, flung him across his back, and staggered across the attic floor. "Alice, are you with me?"

"I'm here," she said.

Struggling blindly, he carried Ike to the top of the stairs. "I don't know if I can do this."

"Just go," said Alice, behind him. "Just go and don't stop."

Fletch nodded, gritted his teeth, and started back down the steep flight of stairs, lurching dangerously from side to side.

One more step.

One more.

Now one more.

Just one more . . .

Somehow, he carried Ike to the second floor.

Not much farther, he told himself.

One more step.

And another . . .

"Alice?" he said.

No reply.

"Alice, are you with me?"

Fletch could hear sirens now—fire engines.

"Alice?"

He stumbled again, and Ike nearly pitched off his back.

One more step.

Another . . .

Suddenly, a pair of arms reached out of the smoke.

"Got you!"

It was Bo Cudhy, and suddenly Fletch sagged.

Then he lost consciousness.

He came to a couple minutes later—lying on the ground outside, staring up at Bo's anxious face.

Around him, he could hear trampling feet, the blat of a police-car radio, voices shouting. A blast of hose water.

Fletch tried to sit up, but his lungs spasmed, and he coughed.

"Hey," said Bo, "just . . . lie still, okay?"

"Ike?"

"He's gonna be okay. You did good, Fletch. You did real good."

Then, "Alice!" Fletch cried.

His face clouding, Bo looked away.

Fletch's blistered hand grabbed Bo's wrist. "Where is Alice?"

Bo shook his head. "She didn't get out," he said.

31

Ike was tumbling into the sun. All around him was a universe of utter blackness, but ahead—dead ahead—was an unimaginably huge ball of raging fire. His skin began to bubble and crisp, then his hair erupted into a torch.

His eyes melted and leaked down over the charred bones of his face.

And yet he was still alive, thrashing in free fall, trying to turn himself around.

Thrashing. . . .

"Whoa, whoa—hey, relax, it's all right!" A woman's voice.

Ike had flung himself up from the mattress, both arms crossing wildly, beating at the air.

Cool, gentle hands took hold of his shoulders and eased him back down onto the bed.

"It's okay," said the voice. "You're in the hospital. Everything's fine, Dwight."

Dwight? Nobody called him Dwight, except—

"Mary?" he said. "Is that you? Dead Mary?"

"Dead Mary?" said the voice, now mixed with a quiet chuckle. "I'm afraid you're still a little bit delirious. My name's Ruth, Dwight. Ruth Hanning."

At last, he focused his eyes, and was staring at a uniformed nurse of about fifty, who stood alongside his bed. Her expression was a mixture of sympathy and amusement. She said, "*Dead* Mary? Must've been quite a delirium."

"I was falling. . . ." He swallowed. "I was falling into the sun."

"Well, I can see where *that* came from," Ruth Hanning replied. She leaned over the bed and drew up the blanket and sheet that Ike had kicked off in his nightmare frenzy. "How are you feeling now, Dwight?"

"I don't know," he said. "Let me think." He lifted his hands and stared at them; they were wrapped thickly in gauze. "How bad? . . ."

"You were very, very lucky, all things considered. Your clothes never caught on fire. *Or* your hair. Quite a miracle."

He nodded, wondering if—if maybe somehow Dead Mary *had* come back. He hadn't seen her, but . . . maybe. How else could he explain it?

"Does it hurt when you breathe?"

"A little."

The nurse nodded. "You swallowed a lot of smoke."

He managed a smile, but abruptly it flattened out as his eyes widened. He just remembered—

"Dwight? What's wrong?"

"The tent!" he said. "Did they get the tent out?"

Nurse Hanning frowned. "I don't know anything about a tent."

"My friends!" he said. "My sister! Where are—"

"Why don't you rest for a little while?" Her eyes looked away, he saw that. There was something she didn't want to tell him.

"What's going on?" he cried. "Where is everybody?! I have to find out—the tent! Where's the tent?"

He moved to fling himself out of bed, but Ruth Hanning took hold of his shoulder. A moment later, he felt a pricking sensation. When he glanced around, he saw the nurse pull free a hypodermic needle from his upper arm.

He laid back down, almost instantly stuporous.

The last thing he noticed before dropping into a dreamless deep sleep, was a small clock on the bedside table: 3:20.

He wondered whether it was the early morning or midafternoon.

And then he was under. . . .

*   *   *

When Ike opened his eyes again, the clock read 7:05. His whole body felt sore and tender—and greasy. Greasy? Some kind of medical salve, he realized. But he hadn't been badly burned, he remembered the nurse telling him that. The nurse, he thought. That was hours ago! What's happened? The tent!

He groaned, lifting his head from the too-soft pillow. Then he opened his eyes, but winced at the overhead rack of fluorescent lights. Lifting a bandaged hand, Ike shielded his face from the glare.

"Hey, Ikester."

"Bo?"

"Right here, babes." Bo was sitting on a chair next to the bed; there was a copy of *People* magazine lying open on his lap. "Can I get you anything? Drink of water?"

"Nothing," said Ike, and with an effort he sat up in bed. "Is it seven in the morning—?"

"Night. It's Monday night."

"Where's—" Ike began, but broke off when Ramona opened the door and stepped into the room.

Seeing Ike awake, she gave him a full smile. Before closing the door behind her, she peeked outside.

Then she put a finger to her lips.

"Whisper," she said. "I don't want that policeman to hear that you're awake."

"What policeman?" said Ike.

"The one who's been waiting around since eight o'clock this morning. They want to question you, Ike, but—" she glanced at Bo—"I thought we should tell you a few things first. So our stories can jibe."

"Do you feel up to talking right now?" asked Bo.

"Yeah, sure. Of course. Now, tell me, what happened? Wait. First tell me this: What about the tent?"

Bo and Ramona exchanged glances. Ramona drew up a chair and sat down. "It's been quite a day," she said.

"The tent!"

154

"Relax, all right? Just let Bo and me give you the lowdown."

Ike bit deeply into his bottom lip and turned his gaze on Bo's anxious face. "If that tent got burnt, we'll never see Del Schofield again."

"Yeah," said Bo, "we figured that out."

"Well?"

One corner of Bo's mouth bent up, and his dimple appeared. "We got it. It's a little scorched, but . . . we got it."

"Where?"

"That's the thing," said Ramona. "That's why we had to talk to you before the cops. We didn't want you telling them anything about any tent. 'Cause they'd want it, wouldn't they? For evidence, or whatever. And Alice said they shouldn't get it, under any circumstances."

"Alice!" said Ike. "Is she—?"

"She's okay." Ramona nodded toward the door. "She's in a room down the hall, as a matter of fact. Right next to Fletch's. It's a regular Jersey convention on this floor."

"Tell me what happened," said Ike.

"It was pretty scary for awhile, there," said Bo. "We thought that Alice was . . . trapped. Fletch—and I don't know how he did it, but he did—Fletch dragged your sorry butt out of that house, Ikester. And he thought Alice was right there behind him, only she wasn't. I tell you, man, scary doesn't even begin to tell the story. And then . . . then the firemen went inside, looking for Alice? But couldn't find her. By then, the whole house was burning. Total loss."

Ramona lifted a hand to silence Bo. Slipping off her chair, she crossed the floor and stood with an ear pressed against the door. She opened it a crack and looked out. "All clear," she said. "I thought I heard somebody coming, but it's okay."

Ike said, "But how did Alice? . . ."

Bo was grinning and shaking his head. "She's something, your big sister. You know that? She pulled up that tent all by herself and carried it outside."

"Alice did?"

"Alice did. 'Cause she seen how crazy you were about saving it—so *she* saved it. And nearly died doing it."

"But how'd she get it out without anybody seeing it?"

"Like I say, man, she's something. She carried it out the *back*—she went out the back door, and managed to drag the damn tent across the yard. She hid it behind that little graveyard. And then she came staggering around the house and practically collapsed. Well, not practically. She did!"

"Is she . . . okay?"

"Some burns—worse than yours, doctor says. And a lot of smoke."

"But you talked to her?"

"Oh, yeah," said Ramona. "I rode in the ambulance with her. And the whole time, she kept whispering to me, 'Tell Ike it's safe.' But she made me promise I wouldn't mention the tent to anybody else."

"And we talked to her again this afternoon," said Bo. "She's doing fine."

"What about Fletch?"

"Up walking around. They're gonna release him tonight."

Ike lay his had back against the pillow, thinking.

"What do the cops make of all this?"

"They think that Jude Hayser kidnaped Del—but they don't know why. And they figure that you went out to the farmhouse and surprised him, and he tied you up and burned the place down and took off with Del."

Ike nodded.

"Hey, by the way—how *did* you get out there?"

"I'm not really sure." When Bo looked at him skeptically, Ike gave a half-shrug, then stroked his chin. "So they're looking for Jude."

"Oh, yeah. It's on the TV every twenty minutes. 'Have-you-seen-this-man,' that kind of thing."

"They won't find him."

Ramona said, "Where *is* he, Ike?" She leaned over, staring

156

intently into his face. "And where's your friend Del? What's going on, really? And the tent, what's that all—?"

"Later," said Ike. "I'll tell you all about it later. But I can tell you this right now: Del isn't anywhere the cops can find her."

There was a light tapping on the door.

Ike squeezed Ramona's hand tightly. "Listen. don't ask questions. Just do what I say. Go back to Hayser's farm. Tonight. Can you do that?"

"Sure. I got my car back."

"Good. So what you have to do, you have to go back to the farm, but don't let anybody see you. And get the tent."

There was another tap on the door, then it opened. Nurse Hanning stuck her head into the room. She scowled when she saw Ramona and Bo. "You shouldn't be in here." Then she glanced behind her and called, "Officer, you can see him for a few minutes now."

Ike sat up, glancing from Ramona to Bo. "Get the tent and take it . . . can you take it to your aunt's house?"

"Sure," said Ramona.

"Okay. Take it there and hide it."

He exhaled and smiled at last.

A plainclothes detective walked in, looked at Ike, and nodded. Then he growled at Ike's visitors, "Out."

As Bo was getting up, Ike turned to him again and whispered, "If you see Alice, tell her thanks."

Bo nodded.

"And tell her—tell her not to eat a thing."

"What?"

"Just tell her that. Not to eat anything."

After Bo and Ramona left, the detective sat down in the chair Ramona had just vacated. He took out a pad and clicked his ballpoint pen. "All right, Mr. Fuelle, let's have it."

He pronounced the name *Foo-well*.

32

At ten minutes to three in the morning, Ike Fuelle, dressed now in wrinkled, pale green O.R. scrubs, slipped quietly into his sister's hospital room.

She was waiting for him.

The lights were off.

"You think we can get out without anybody seeing us?" Alice whispered.

"Pretty sure. It's dead out there now on the floor. I seen one nurse way down at the other end—reading a magazine. We can do it." He passed her a scrub shirt and a pair of drawstring pants.

The clothing they'd worn to the hospital had been deemed too badly burned and scorched to be salvaged.

While Alice dressed hurriedly, Ike stepped to the window and peered through the narrow blinds. He could look down into the parking lot behind the hospital. There weren't more than a dozen cars there. One of them was Ramona's Mitsubishi. The headlights were on, according to Ike's instructions.

He'd hatched this little escape plan shortly after his interrogation by the Richmond police detective. Lieutenant Parker had been less than satisfied by Ike's story, and he'd kept pushing Ike, saying, "Now wait a second, *how* did you get all the way out to that farm? *Why* did Mr. Hayser decide to burn his house down?" Ike had pleaded wooziness, the aftereffects of all that smoke inhalation, and the detective finally snapped his notebook closed. But he'd be back in the morning, he promised. And he made it clear that Ike had better have his story straight.

Ike had decided to skip the hospital before he had to talk any more about Jude Hayser.

When, a little before ten o'clock, Ramona Pruitt phoned Ike to say that she and Bo and Fletch had retrieved that "little item" he was so concerned about, Ike had told her to meet Alice and himself in the parking lot, at three on the dot. . . .

"Ready," Alice said now.

Ike turned from the blinds. "Okay." But before they left the room, he gripped his sister by the shoulders. "Are you feeling okay?"

"I'm all right. You?"

"Not bad." His face and hands (he'd unwrapped and discarded the bandages before coming down here) were still stinging painfully, and his lungs felt carbonized, but he couldn't let himself think about any of that too much. "Alice? Thanks for . . . you know. Saving that tent."

"Ikey? Did you . . . did you see Mary Dunham? Is that how you got out to the farm?"

"Uh-huh."

"That's what I figured. Well, let's get going."

"Alice—you know what we both have to do, don't you?"

"Oh, yeah. Yeah, I do. Since we qualify, we're elected."

Ike nodded. "Two orphans. A male and a female."

She reached a hand to his face and stroked his cheek. "We'll get her back."

Ike said nothing. He just opened the door, looked both ways down the hospital corridor, and said, "Coast is clear. Come on."

They took the fire stairs.

Four minutes later, they were dashing barefoot across the parking lot.

Fletch jumped from the back of the Mirage and held the door open for them both to climb in. "Okay," he said, once he'd gotten back in himself and slammed the door. "We're outta here."

Ramona made a wide U-turn, punched the accelerator, and shot the car across the deserted parking lot, taking the speed-bumps way too fast.

Grinning, Bo knelt up on the front passenger seat, looked at Ike and Alice, and gave a thumbs-up.

Ike almost made one of his typically caustic remarks; he nearly said to Bo, What are *you* so happy about?

Instead, he bit his tongue and turned to Fletch.

"I never got a chance to thank you," he said. "Thanks, man. You, um, you saved my life."

Ike Fuelle expressing gratitude? Whoa. Fletch looked flabbergasted, was dumbfounded for several moments. Then he nodded. "You're just lucky you don't weigh more. Otherwise, you were barbecue."

Aunt Ardeth, in her Chinese bathrobe again, popped out her front door the second the car pulled into her driveway. Her eyes grew saucer-wide when Ike and Alice climbed from the backseat wearing scrub clothes.

"I bet I know what *she's* thinking," Bo whispered to Ramona. "Crazy Yankees."

"And can you blame her?"

"Nope."

Several hours earlier, on the way back through Richmond, after retrieving the tent from Jude Hayser's family graveyard, Ramona had suggested to Fletch and Bo that they clear out their rooms at the Holiday Inn, settle the bill, and move, for the time being, into her aunt's house. It seemed like good idea then, and it seemed an even better one now, at almost four in the morning. Nobody expected to catch any sleep in the foreseeable future, but at least Ike and Alice could put on their own clothes. Which is what they did just as soon as they got into the house.

Aunt Ardeth suggested they might like to take showers, but they declined. It would have been great to scrub the smoke reek from their hair, but their skin was still far too raw to even consider standing under a spray of water.

After they'd changed into fresh T-shirts and jeans, they joined the others in the kitchen.

Aunt Ardeth had brewed a pot of coffee and put out a

platter of donuts. Ike took one look at those—his favorite kind: chocolate-covered—and suffered a hunger pang. But he refused to eat, and Alice—after catching his cautioning expression—also passed.

Ike suspected—actually, he hoped and prayed—that Jude Hayser's two-week fast had been done more from a sense of, well, tradition than anything else. The Orphan Thomas had done it, so Jude would, too.

And if Ike was wrong about that? If fasting was intrinsic to the Migration? Then what? Then big trouble, that's what. Because he couldn't imagine being able to wait fourteen days before he and Alice used the tent.

He could deal with the hunger, but the anxiety about Del would kill him.

Already he was eager to get going.

Ike realized now, as he took a seat at the kitchen table, that everyone had fallen silent (even Aunt Ardeth!) and was staring at him. His move.

Taking a long breath, then letting it out slowly, he leaned forward on his elbows. "You guys want to know what's going on. Okay. In a nutshell, Jude Hayser's tent—where is it, by the way?"

"In the backyard," said Fletch.

"I wouldn't have it smelling up my house," said Aunt Ardeth.

"Fine," said Ike. "Okay. Jude Hayser's tent is actually some kind of . . . doorway. That's what he called it. A doorway or gateway to—to some other place. Don't ask me where, don't ask me how. But sixty years ago, all those orphans we've been hearing about used tents just like it to move from here to . . . there. And last night, Jude used his to do the same thing. And he took Del with him."

Aunt Ardeth shot a look at her niece. It said, Who *are* these people? They're not *really* friends of yours, are they?

"So we're gonna go pitch that tent," said Fletch, "and use it ourselves. Okay. Let's do it." He was rising from his chair when Alice lifted a hand and waved him back down.

Fletch hesitated, then sat again.

"We're going to pitch it, that's right," Alice said. "But you're not going into it. Just Ike. And me."

"Bull!" said Fletch.

Alice smiled. "I wish you *could* come. But you can't."

"Why?"

Alice's smile curved higher. " 'Cause you've got a mom who loves you."

"What?"

Bo slapped the table. "Oh, man!" he said. "Now I get the deal! Orphans only, huh? *That's* why Jude was so interested in Ramona at first. The creep!"

Aunt Ardeth's gaze kept bouncing from face to face; her lips were moving, but she wasn't saying a thing. She'd turned exceedingly pale. Ike could read her expression: Creep? Interested in Ramona, *her* Ramona? What on earth was everybody *talking* about?

"Alice? I don't want you to go," said Fletch.

"You think I want to? But how else are we supposed to find Del?" She turned to her brother. "Are you about ready?"

"I've *been* ready."

The wall tent, scorched black and peppered with burn holes, some the size of pinpricks, others ragged and gaping, lay in a crumpled heap on the ground in the small, freshly mowed backyard. The tent poles were bundled inside it.

While Ramona searched in the basement for some rope to replace the charred and useless guy-lines, Bo, Fletch, and Ike unrolled the canvas, figured out which pole went where, and hoisted the tent.

Standing inside it as they adjusted the roof pole, Ike nearly gagged on the odor of smoke.

This isn't going to work, he suddenly thought with a blast of panic. It's not! It won't work.

When he stepped back outside, Alice saw the despair etched in his face. And read his mind.

"We're gonna find her, Ikey." Then, with a little grin, she corrected herself: "Ike."

"Yeah," he said. "We are."

He just wished he believed it.

At last, with fresh rope stretched taut from the sides and the pegs driven into the ground, the tent was fully erected.

Ike's mouth went dry.

"What . . . happens now?" said Bo.

"I guess we just . . . I don't *know* what happens now," Ike replied. "We go in and then—I hope—we come out someplace else."

He looked at Alice.

She stepped toward the tent, then stopped. Suddenly she turned, ran over to Fletch, and hugged him once. Then flinging herself away, she grabbed Ike's hand, and together they ducked inside the Orphan's tent.

The flaps swished closed behind them.

Fletch looked at his wristwatch: 4:25.

Then 4:26.

. . . 4:27.

Suddenly, "Are all you people *insane*?" bellowed aunt Ardeth. "I think I've been very patient with you all, but I've finally had quite enough! She turned her face toward the tent and called, "You two in there! Come out and stop this nonsense right now. I will not have that unsightly thing standing in my backyard for another min—"

"Ardeth, please," said Ramona, sharply—so sharply that her aunt recoiled. Her spine stiffened.

But she didn't speak another word.

Bo glanced at Fletch, then called, "You guys? Ike? Alice?" He reached for the tent flaps, grabbed, one, and timidly pulled it open.

The tent was vacant.

33

Because Ike Fuelle had experienced a crisis of faith and nerve (suddenly he was icy positive that he'd open the flaps to find just Bo, Fletch, Ramona, and dotty Aunt Ardeth staring back at him, slack-jawed), his sister Alice was the first to set foot outside.

It was another world, all right.

"Ike! You gotta see this! Come on!"

By the time Ike summoned enough courage to leave the tent, Alice had already wandered off a short distance, and was hunkered by the edge of a precipitous granite cliff. Raveled out below, far below, and stretched to an unimaginably distant horizon, lay green forested land stitched with rivers and dotted with blue lakes. She breathed in deeply, filling her achy lungs with the freshest, and positively the sweetest, air that she'd ever tasted. Ever.

Glancing around, she waved impatiently to Ike—come closer and look!

He came, but he took his time getting there. His eyes were narrowed skeptically, and with every step that he took through the high, spiky (and vaguely perfumed) saw grass, he seemed baffled not to be in dire jeopardy—amazed that the loamy ground beneath his feet hadn't opened and swallowed him whole.

"Is this place beautiful, or what?" Alice kept shaking her head in reverential awe. "Look at those clouds!" She pointed, but Ike barely raised his eyes.

He had a serious case of crawling skin.

"Ike, look down there, see how that river winds around like a—"

"Alice! Quit with the travelogue, would you? Next thing,

164

you'll be wishing you brought along a camera. We're here to find Del, remember? And so far I don't see any trace of her. Or anybody else, for that matter."

"Well . . ."

Disgusted, Ike flung an arm toward the aboriginal forest spread below them. "They could be anyplace. Her and Jude."

Alice straightarmed her brother, knocking him in the shoulder with the heel of her hand and throwing him off balance. "You're whining again, Ikey. And there I'd thought you'd changed."

"I'm just saying."

"Yeah, yeah." She took a final, appreciative survey of the landscape, then trudged across the grassy mountain cliff back toward the tent. "Well, let's get this thing down and rolled up. Then I guess we'll just . . . pick a direction. And go."

She squatted beside a tent peg, gripped its head in both hands, and, leaning back on her heels, pulled. When it slid free of the earth, she dropped it and moved laterally in a duckwalk to the next one.

The tent sagged toward the center pole.

Ike said, "You really think we should take it down?"

"You want to leave it here? I don't think so. Give me a hand, all right?"

Twisting his mouth to one side, Ike considered. Yeah. Alice was right. Where we go, it goes. The tent comes with us.

He grabbed the front pole and, gritting his teeth, yanked it up, then slid it, like a canoe paddle, toward him. The canvas drooped, and the tent lost its shape.

In Aunt Ardeth's backyard, as the first glimmer of dawn touched the sky over Richmond, Bo Cudhy was lifting a mug to his mouth. His hand froze suddenly in midair with such a jerk that hot coffee splashed out.

"Hey!"

Everyone else had gone into the house. It was Bo's watch.

165

He'd only taken his eyes off the tent for a minute, no longer, but now—

"Fletch!" he shouted. "Ramona!"

The kitchen door banged open.

"What?" said Fletch. "What's—?"

The tent shivered and fluttered, and like the afterimage of a glorious firework on July Fourth, it faded—sparkling, glimmering, and flaring for one final instant, then gone.

Ramona slumped against the door jamb, a hand clapped to her mouth.

Behind her, in the kitchen, Aunt Ardeth peeked out. Then her eyebrows jumped. "Where did it *go?*" she asked, her voice hushed. "Ramona? Where did it go?"

Bo was hunkered down now where the tent had stood till just thirty seconds ago. He poked a finger into a peg hole, then pulled it out and stared quizzically at his fingertip. He glanced up at Fletch, who was standing there with an agonized expression on his face.

Bo said, "Do you think—?"

"I'm way past that," said Fletch. "Thinking? Forget about it. Right now," he said, "I'm just praying."

They rolled the tent as tightly compact as they could get it, then lashed it around with guy-lines. And now, as they picked their way carefully down a stony—but, thank God, gradually sloped—mountainside, walking single file, they carried it between them. The weight was evenly distributed on each of their left shoulders. Dangling pegs clinked in rhythm.

The temperature seemed to be about seventy-five degrees, and the breeze was lightly rose-scented. But they didn't see any roses—just thousands upon thousands of gray, waist-high pussywillows. Those things grew everywhere.

They hadn't noticed birds of any sort, and the only insects appeared to be a variety of queerly iridescent gnat. Clouds of them would appear, swirl in a mad airborne dance, then move off.

Ike halted so abruptly that Alice almost walked right into him. "Listen!" he whispered and gestured toward a thicket festooned with tiny berries—red-purple and dark green.

The brush shook violently.

Alice drew a breath and held it.

A small, bristly animal about seven or eight inches long burst from the thicket, then stopped dead. Its snout jutted into the air, its black, moist nostrils quivered furiously, and its eyes—all six of them, all red but for a creamy white one—focused on Ike. Then it spun around on little sharp-toed feet and shot back into the bushes.

"Did you see how many—?"

"I saw, Ike. I saw."

It was definitely another world, all right.

He blew out a noisy breath. "Ready?"

"Ready," said Alice.

They trudged on.

Behind them, a green filament, one inch wide, wriggled up from the cracked earth. Moments later, another appeared. Then another. One more. One more. Still another. In less than a minute, nearly forty had punched their way from the dirt and were growing taller, sprouting bristles, thickening. Worm-size. Snake-width. Eel. As they grew—matured—they each leaned toward a common center, where they merged, one closing into the other, into the other, till there was only a single stalk with the girth of a saguaro cactus and roots by the score. It jutted six feet—seven feet, eight, nine—into the air. It pulsed wildly in a dozen areas up and down the shaft.

Then it flopped forward, whipping itself from side to side until, root by root, it snapped completely free of the earth.

It slithered forward, moving very fast.

Tracking.

"Can we stop for a while?"

Ike said, "Yeah, all right," making it sound as begrudging

167

as he could, although for the past ten minutes he'd been desperate for a rest break himself.

They both leaned sharply leftward at the same time, letting the bundled tent drop from their shoulders and hit the ground with a clanking thud.

"We should've thought to bring something to eat," said Alice.

"Yeah. I know. And it would've been nice to have some kind of weapon. We should've thought of *that,* too."

"We were in a hurry."

Ike nodded. "Yeah. But that still doesn't excuse us."

"No," Alice replied with a small, tired smile.

They sprawled out on their backs in soft grass and stared at the sky. It seemed all speeded up, the clouds whizzing past like special effects in a movie.

"I'm really starving," said Alice.

"Don't think about it."

Alice plucked a blade of grass, nibbled it.

"You know what I'm wondering?" said Ike after a while.

"No. But I'd love to."

He turned his head slightly and scowled at her. Was she goofing on him? Teasing? No, Alice stared levelly back at him.

"I'm wondering . . . what happened to all those people we saw. The ones from 1934."

"Yeah, I've been wondering that myself."

"Sixty years."

"Long time. Yeah. And you'd think by now they'd've built some . . . I don't know . . . villages or something."

"There must be a lot *more* of them by this time."

"I was thinking that, too."

"So?"

"Yeah. So where *is* everybody?"

"Of course—they could all be on the other side of the world."

Alice sat up. "What?"

"Well, if this is a *world* . . ."

168

"Oh my God! They could be, like—"

"In Asia, so to speak. While you and me, we're traipsing around South America. So to speak."

"Or Europe. Oh, man, Ikey. You're right! But Del . . . *she'd* have to be nearby, right?"

"We're assuming things we don't know anything about."

Alice drew her knees to her chest and hugged them. "So what are you suggesting? That we just pitch our magic tent and go home? Now?"

Ike rose slowly to his feet. "Nah. Let's keep looking. For awhile." He reached down and pulled Alice up. "Okay?"

"Okay," she said and laughed.

"What's so funny?"

"Nothing."

"No, what? Tell me."

"Well, it's not funny, it's just—you *have* changed, Ike. You're different. The old Ike for sure would've said let's go home."

"And that made you laugh?"

"No. I laughed because that made me happy."

Ike blushed, then made a surly, bearish face. "Let's get on our way, huh?"

As they were hefting the tent back onto their shoulders, a single, high-pitched, almost keening wheeze shattered the silence. Brush snapped somewhere above and behind them. The ground thrummed, and the vibration shot through the soles of their sneakers. Then, glancing around, glimpsing the huge green—slug? worm? monster!—Ike shouted, "Run!"

But it slithered far too fast.

Before Alice could even start to flee, its blunt, horny cigar-shaped head slammed into the small of her back, drilling her flesh, instantly, with hundreds of tiny bristles. Stingers. Her muscles cramped in bundles, and she screamed. Alice's body jerked spastically. Then she hit the ground, a dead weight. And was knocked out cold.

The monster's blunt head split open, vertically, top to bottom, with a loud, tearing sound.

It had teeth inside. Big teeth.

That's what Ike saw, when he looked behind him, to make sure that Alice was still with him. Those teeth. Dozens of them, in curving rows—predator's teeth in a mouth the size of a tractor-trailer tire, a mouth that was set to tear his sister in half.

Two thoughts passed through Ike's mind while he ran back: one, he *really* wished that he'd brought along some kind of weapon; and two, he really, *really* wished that Del Schofield had never, repeat never, come into his life.

As he flung himself upon the slug-thing, worm-thing, snake-thing, *whatever*, Ike thought:

I'm gonna die.

I love Del.

Then a quiver of stingers punctured his arms, fingers, throat, and chest, and his mind blacked out.

34

At most, Ike was unconscious for half a minute. Then his eyelids snapped wide open and stayed wide open; he couldn't close them. Nor could he move any other muscles.

His eyes were fixed rigidly, his vision was a jittery murk. Then it cleared, and he could see. But he still couldn't move. Don't let me be paralyzed—please!

That became Ike's frenzied mantra, repeated over and over in his head, as he watched a dozen or more naked, snarly-haired men and women hack away with stone knives at the carcass of the . . . whatever it was. Ike thought it looked most like a giant slug. A giant green slug. It was tubular and actually tapered, when you saw it from a distance.

He was lying flat on his back, peering down his belly and between his feet, watching the wild-looking people (some as young as twelve or thirteen, others as old as fifty) carve up the slug. Somebody would cut off a large steak and toss it to somebody else, who would lay it carefully into a reed basket.

Don't let me be paralyzed. . . .

Gradually, Ike detected a slight tingling in his toes and in his fingertips, then he could feel blood start to flow again up his legs and down his arms. Then he could blink. Then he could sit up. Standing, though, wasn't such a good idea; he tried, but his knees gave out, and he sat down, hard.

A little girl of about seven—blond and slender, with dirty hands and knees—suddenly noticed Ike. She bent forward, studying him.

"Old Penrad!" she called, her voice pitched strangely high, almost falsetto. "Old Penrad!"

An elderly man who'd been watching the slug butchers turned in response. He was bald, and a large brown mole

172

jutted out just above his left eyebrow. His flesh was wrinkled and bagged, but he had sinewy arms and heavy-muscled calves. He smiled when the little girl pointed to Ike.

When he came closer, he maintained his smile, and Ike could see that the few teeth he still had left in his mouth were black and stubby.

"How are ye feelin', Bo?" he asked.

"I'd feel better if I could stand up."

"Give it a minute. Stalk poison takes a little time to wear off."

"Stalk?"

"That big succulent plant over there. That's a Stalk."

"It's a plant? Not a slug?"

"What it is, sonny, is a blade of *grass*. And it tastes good after a couple of days, too. Well, not good. It tastes all right. It keeps you alive, is what it does. Now, take it slow, sonny boy. Here, let me help you."

The old man went quickly to Ike's side and gripped his left elbow. As soon as Ike had his balance, though, and was standing, he freed himself. The guy reeked of dried sweat.

"Did you, I mean all of you, did you *kill* that thing?"

"Just like regular cavemen," said the old man, and laughed heartily. Then he clapped Ike on the shoulder. "Tell me something—where did you get the tent?"

"It's—"

"No, before you tell me that, tell me this: Did the Great Depression ever end?"

"Yeah," said Ike. "I'm pretty sure." History had never been Ike's strongest subject. The Depression was what—that time when you couldn't drink legally? Elliot Ness, Al Capone, speakeasies. Wasn't that the Great Depression? "Yeah," said Ike, "you can buy beer in any supermarket."

The old man gave him a startled look.

"But my sister could tell you better than me," Ike added, when he saw Alice come wobbling from around the far side of the Stalk and lift a trembly hand and wave.

*   *   *

The old man, whose name was Jack Penrad ("But just call me Old Penrad," he said. "Everybody does."), was eager to hear all about FDR and the Second World War and television, and Alice was only too glad to fill him in as best as she could on sixty years of American history, but—

"But can't we talk about all that another time?" she finally said. "We're looking for somebody—maybe you can help us find her."

They were gathered now inside the smoky recesses of a fairly complex and roomy series of caverns. Old Penrad wasn't kidding about his companions being regular cavemen.

They'd gone there—the cavern wasn't a far hike—as soon as the Stalk had been carved clean and packed away in baskets. A couple of the butchers (salad chefs?) had carried the tent, which Ike was nervous about. He'd insisted on walking behind the tent-bearers; he wanted to keep an eye on it.

Counting the dozen who'd been with Old Penrad and probably another fifteen or so back in the cave, Ike and Alice had seen less than thirty people. Several dogs sniffed them avidly when they arrived.

The implements—axes, knives, spears—they'd spotted lying around looked like artists' renderings of Cro-Magnon life in some book about "Our First Ancestors." Low stools and benches were the only furniture. Apparently, these people slept on thick mattings of brown grass.

Old Penrad asked now, "Who are you looking for?"

"A girl and a guy," said Ike. "Dressed like us. Dressed, period. Speaking of that—how come nobody here wears any clothes?"

"We haven't discovered a clothing tree yet."

"You mean you don't . . . sew or anything?" said Alice.

"Sew with what? Who has fabric? Who has thread? When we got here, we were the first people. Where do you start? How do you grow cotton? How do you make looms? Would *you* know how? I don't think we did so badly, all things considered."

"Are the people here . . . all that's left?"

"Are you kidding?" said Old Penrad. "Girl, there are probably *hundreds* of us by now. A couple thousand, maybe. Scattered all over the place."

174

"You mean you didn't stick together?" said Ike. "I thought that was the whole idea. No families, just—"

Old Penrad clicked his few teeth and drew his lips back into a huge grin. "That was Dunbar's idea. But Dunbar didn't last two days. He was the first to get swallowed by a Stalk. No, I guess he was the second. A woman was first."

"Of course," said Alice.

Old Penrad gave her a quizzical look.

She waved it away. "So you people split up?"

"Into clans. But not right away. It took awhile. At first we just had to find some way to keep alive. This is one hellacious place our Brother-Orphan Tom Dunbar brought us all to, let me tell you."

"But it looks so beautiful," said Alice. "Except for that stalky-thing," she amended.

"That 'stalky-thing,'" said Old Penrad, "makes life a miserable experience ninety percent of the time. You can't stop it from growing, they're everywhere. I guess when Dunbar scouted this place for us, he didn't see any of *those* things."

"No weed-killers, huh?" said Ike.

"Don't be a smart-aleck, kid. They're not funny. You stick around, you'll see. Well, you've *seen* already."

Old Penrad looked up then, glancing past Ike to nod at a woman, about forty years old, who'd come silently into the cavern. Ike looked around at her, then glanced away fast. She didn't have any clothes on. But seeing her wasn't like seeing a picture in *Playboy*. It was like seeing a picture in *National Geographic*.

"I'll be with you in a moment, Eleanor," Old Penrad told the woman. She folded her arms and leaned against a rock. It gleamed black with fire soot.

Old Penrad turned back to Ike and Alice. "So, to answer your question, no, we're not one big happy family of orphans. There are several different clans. Some we get along with, others we don't. But we don't fight or anything—except with the Tomsons. And we *all* fight with the Tomsons."

"The Tomsons?" said Alice.

"Sons of Thomas. The Tomsons," said Old Penrad. "They invented their own religion. They sacrifice people to the Stalks. But naturally they prefer to sacrifice people who aren't Tomsons. Which is what all the fighting's about."

"You're kidding me," said Ike.

"What's your name—Spike? I wouldn't kid about that, Spike. They do it."

"Ike. My name is Ike."

Old Penrad flipped his hand casually. Spike, Ike, what did it matter?

"But what's the point?" said Alice.

"Of what?" asked Old Penrad.

"The point of sacrificing people!"

"Oh. The Tomsons want to reinvent agriculture. They want to be farmers. But there's no way you can do that when every field you try to clear just grows a hundred Stalks every day that gobble you up. So they're trying to make a deal with the Stalks. They'll treat the Stalks like gods, if the Stalks will just leave them alone."

"Any luck?" said Ike.

"What do you think? It's a daft idea—but then, that's what the Tomsons are: completely daft."

". . . Getting back to Del," said Alice.

"Del? Who's Del?"

"The girl we're looking for."

"Haven't seen any girl wearing clothes," said Old Penrad. "And, believe me, I'd have remembered."

"That's why I wanted to talk to you," said the woman who'd been waiting patiently with her arms crossed. "The Tomsons have her. A Dunbarite just came from the valley, saying that. The Tomsons found dressed people. Two of them."

Old Penrad winced and pressed a hand to his midriff, as if against a sudden strafe of pain.

"That's not good news," he said, turning to Alice. "What I mean is, you two have yourselves a big problem."

35

"I'll bet he must be one of the last original orphans," said Alice. "From 1934—the ones who came in the tents."

"Yeah. So he's one of the last originals. So what?"

"I'm only making conversation, Ike."

"Is that really necessary? Considering what we're trying to do right now, and considering where we are. . . ."

"All right, all right," she said irritably.

At the moment, they were lying flat on their stomachs on a jutting ledge, about a hundred feet above the Tomsons' sacrificial altar, a grassy clearing encircled by thick forest.

A party of Old Penrad's younger cave-mates (two men and a woman in their twenties, though their eyes looked older) had led Alice and Ike to this place. And left them there. They'd have to get back to the cave on their own. Either with or without Del.

The sky was turning an ashy gray. Just over the trees, the descending sun was a red ball.

Ike didn't know if he could find his way back in the dark. He was worried about that, and he was also worried about the tent.

He wanted to take it along with them, but it was too bulky. If—by some miracle—they managed to rescue Del (if she hadn't already been eaten by a hungry blade of dinosaur grass), they'd have to move quickly. Run like hell. Dragging the tent would just slow them down. The Tomsons might even get hold of it.

Yeah, they *had* to leave the tent behind in the cavern with Old Penrad.

Still, Ike would have felt a lot more secure having it along with him.

"You know what?" Alice suddenly whispered. "I just realized!"

"What? What now?" His eyes were glued on the clearing. Still no sign of anybody coming there. "What?"

"Old Penrad? I saw him once before. When I was back in that field, in 1934. Only he was a little kid then, a little boy. He bumped into me."

"That's fascinating, Alice," said Ike. "But I asked you to be quiet."

"Shhh!" she replied, her eyes widening. Then she pointed down.

Struggling, their arms pinned behind them, Del Schofield and Jude Hayser emerged from the treeline, roughly escorted forward by a cluster of mud-daubed men and women. Delivered to the altar place, they were flung to the ground, then lashed to pegs by their ankles and wrists.

"It's like *King Kong*," said Ike. He knew it was a stupid thing to say, and it *wasn't* funny, this was serious, but he couldn't resist. "It's like what they did to Fay Wray in *King Kong!*"

"Shhh!" said Alice.

Old Dunbar had told them what to expect: the victims would be tied down, a high priest would make a solemn invocation, then the Tomsons would all withdraw to the safety of their own caves. Apparently they never stuck around to watch—they were too afraid the unpredictable Stalks would turn on them, rather than accept the living offering they'd prepared.

Alice hoped there'd be no change in the ceremony today.

A rawboned, towering man with an enormous shock of red hair separated from the crowd of Tomsons and walked forward toward the two bound victims. When he spoke, his voice carried clearly up to Alice and Ike, but his language was a garble of English and something new. They couldn't understand much of what he said. The gist of it seemed to be that Del and Jude Hayser ought to feel proud they'd been selected to die, and the clan would forever value their contribution . . . at every future harvest.

Ike muttered, "Yeah. Right."

Alice shifted to whisper something in his ear, but as she

moved, she dislodged a loose stone; it rolled, then fell over the ledge.

Ike's hand shot out and caught it. Carefully, he put it back. He rolled his eyes in relief, then narrowed them, censuring Alice for her clumsiness. She ignored that and said in a low voice, "When they're gone, I'll take Del, you take Jude."

"What're you *talking* about?" Ike replied in a fierce whisper. "I'm not cutting him loose. He can stay and get eaten. And if I wasn't in such a rush and didn't want to maybe get eaten myself, I'd stay and watch."

"Then *I'll* cut him loose," said Alice. Her jaw had gone rigid, and her eyes blazed. "I'm not leaving him."

"All right, all right."

"I can't believe you *said* that."

"All right, already. Enough. Now will you shut up?"

Just as Old Penrad had told them would happen, the Tomsons cut and ran.

"Let's go," said Alice, and before the words were even out of her mouth, she and Ike slipped over the ledge and went sliding down the hillside feet first, stones shooting away from their sneakers.

Green filaments were already wriggling up in a dozen places around the clearing.

Ike propelled himself to his feet and into a sprint.

He took Del. Slashing with a sharp stone knife that he borrowed at the cavern, he cut the bindings at her wrists. He looked at Del once, but had to look away immediately. She seemed . . . dazed, out of her head. Her eyes looked feverish. Her face was raw with fresh scratches and scabs.

He cut Del's feet bindings, then helped her stand up. She was nodding now, nodding and watching her legs wobble under her. "Can you walk?" Ike said.

She nodded again. Then she flinched, and Ike saw five or six thickening filaments quaver alongside her foot.

He stomped on them and kept stomping.

Alice jerked him by the arm. "Stop it! Don't waste your time. We're leaving!"

When Ike saw Jude Hayser standing three feet away, looking more than a little dazed himself, rubbing his wrists, he felt a spasm of rage.

"Ikey! No!"

But he pushed past Alice, grabbed Jude by his shirt, and punched him on the side of his face.

Jude staggered, then his head snapped forward. He shook it once and looked directly at Ike.

Ike was startled by Jude's expression; it conveyed abysmal shame and regret.

Jude opened his mouth, but right away Ike thrust up a hand. "Don't say anything. Don't even say a word. We'll talk later, you bastard. Right now—you just follow us and don't get separated. 'Cause I'm not coming back for you." He took Del's wrist and led her across the clearing.

"We have to climb—can you do it?"

Del pulled her arm free. "Do I look helpless to you?" she snapped, and Ike, for the first time, believed they might actually come out of this nightmare alive.

He'd found Del, and she was the same Del that he'd gone looking for.

Two minutes later:

"I think we go left here."

"I think we go *right*."

"Left," said Ike.

"You're sure?"

"I'm sure."

Alice nodded. They went Ike's way, to the right.

And got lost.

"I *told* you!" she said ten minutes later, when it became obvious.

"Alice, what do you want me to say?"

It was almost dark by now, and in the heavy forest the gloom was so thick they were beginning to walk into trees and to stumble over deadfall and thick roots.

"This way?" said Ike.

"It's as good as any," said Alice. Her voice was steely with aggravation. And fear. She was scared out of her wits. What if they couldn't find their way back? What if they got separated? That thought set her off. "Ike?" She reached a hand behind her and touched nothing. "Ike? Del?"

"I'm right here," said Del.

When Alice turned, she couldn't see her. But then Del touched her hand, and in relief Alice squeezed it.

But, "Where's Ike?" she said then. "And Jude?"

They called and got a distant response from Ike. "I can hear you guys!" he yelled. "Where *are* you?"

Jude Hayser didn't answer their call.

He'd vanished.

"I'm over here!" Ike hollered, with both hands cupped around his mouth. "Follow my voice! Alice? Del?"

He decided not to move—just to keep shouting until they followed his voice to him. He leaned against a tree.

But the tree reared back and gave off a piercingly high wheezing sound.

Madly, Ike brushed at his arm, but it was already stinging in half a dozen places. He began to feel muscle cramps in his fingers.

His right hand flexed open and his knife dropped.

He lost coordination and fell.

Somebody's hand closed firmly around his wrist. And then Ike was being dragged, his stomach and left side abraded by stones, his legs swiveling behind him.

Finally the hand let go, and Ike lay in heavy brush. Paralyzed again, he stared fixedly into darkness; several moments passed and then Jude's face loomed up large in front of him. "I'm sorry," he said.

That's all, "I'm sorry."

And then Jude Hayser was gone.

Ike heard a loud thrashing, tree branches cracking off, another wheeze, Jude's loud grunt, then a tearing sound.

Followed, seconds later, by an earth-pounding thud.

36

When Del and Alice pitched the tent in Old Penrad's personal chamber in the clan's cavern, everybody came to see it. The old bald man was, as Alice had suspected, the last of the original orphans, but the entire clan, naturally, had heard about the Migration. And now here was an actual tent, and not just *any* tent, it was the Orphan Thomas's. The First Tent. A piece of their history.

Children kept touching it and putting their fingers through different burn holes.

Nobody went inside, though.

They peeked through the flaps, but nobody went inside.

Old Penrad explained why. "They're afraid they might come out in the *other* place. *Your* world."

Ike, who was lying on a bed of straw, said, "I thought they'd *want* to go back."

"Why? *This* is where they live. Would you go to Mars?"

"Yeah, but—those Stalks."

Old Penrad laughed. "Alice was telling me a few things before. We have Stalks, you have drive-by shootings. We're all most comfortable with what we know best."

Del, squatted on her heels at Ike's bedside, nodded musingly. Ike caught that. He lifted a quizzical eyebrow, and she said, "I'm just thinking, that's the truth. When Jude first told me about another world, I said, Yeah! But when I thought about it? I thought, no way, I'll take what I have. Only Jude wouldn't let me change my mind. . . ."

At the mention of Jude's name, Ike felt a bright, confusing mixture of emotions. He despised Jude Hayser. Despised him. And yet he owed the guy his life.

Jude had pulled him away from that Stalk, then had gone

back and—what? Tried to fight it? Lead it away? Offered himself as a diversion? Whatever he'd tried to do—unless it was to commit suicide—he had failed.

When Old Penrad and a search party found Ike just after daylight (what a horrendous several hours *that* had been), they'd also found fresh blood nearby, but no trace of either Jude Hayser or the Stalk.

Old Penrad's chuckling voice, right next to his ear, brought Ike out of his sorrowful but oddly satisfied reverie. "You're welcome to stay with us, of course."

"No, thanks," said Ike, and the old man roared his laughter, eyes teasing and merry.

"Suit yourself," he said. "Ready to go, then? Need a hand up?"

"I can stand by myself," said Ike, testily.

Del laughed, and Alice shook her head in mock disgust.

Old Penrad's clanspeople stood by and watched with great curiosity as the three *dressed* orphans walked to the tent. Before they entered, Alice turned to nod in parting to everyone (Ike was amazed that their nakedness didn't seem to faze her). Then to Old Penrad she said, "I think you ought to take down the tent right after we leave—don't you? And keep it? Start a museum or something?"

"Are you trying to make us civilized, Sister?" He laughed again and touched Alice's shoulder fondly. She kissed him, a peck on the cheek. He shook hands with Ike and then with Del.

"We don't even know that this is going to work," said Ike. "There are three of us now—and it's in reverse. It probably won't work!"

Alice shoved him into the tent. "Quit being a pessimist, would you?"

Del was the last one in.

It was Fletch, just half an hour before, who'd gone out into the backyard and discovered that the tent had reappeared. He'd called for the others, and since then they'd been sitting vigil. Even Aunt Ardeth, who kept bringing out trays of sandwiches and tumblers of iced tea.

"How come it came back, do you think?" Bo said now.

Nobody had spoken for several minutes, and the sound of Bo's voice startled everyone.

"How come it disappeared in the first place?" said Ramona.

"I think they took it down when they got there," said Fletch. "And I think they just put it back up again."

"So they should be coming," said Bo. "Like, any second now." He paused, then added, "This is like waiting for a train."

Fletch scowled, but Ramona smiled. That's what counted. Who cared about Fletch?

"Hey!" said Del Schofield's voice from inside the tent.

She was the first one out.

Epilogue

On the Friday morning after their return to Jerseyville, a visitor came to Alice's music shop.

She was doing some paperwork at the front counter while Fletch opened several UPS deliveries and entered CD titles and T-shirt counts into the store's computer. He was working at We Got It now. Because he hadn't shown up for work at Allen's Garage on Monday or Tuesday, he'd been fired. Alice felt so responsible that she'd offered Fletch a job. He'd accepted only because he liked the idea of being with her all the time. Already they were talking about expanding the business. Maybe opening a larger store. Or a second store.

But first, they'd decided, they'd get Ike's music label launched.

The label was now called WE GOT IT RECORDS.

Ike Fuelle, President.

Alice Fuelle, Vice-President.

Steve Fletcher, Director of Marketing.

Del Schofield, Talent. Hit-maker.

They hoped.

That morning, when the visitor came by, Ike was in a small storage room at the rear of the store. He was listening to Del's kitchen-made tapes, deciding which four songs he'd suggest that she record next week in a Philadelphia studio.

The tiny bell over the front door jingled.

Alice looked up from her scratchpad.

"Danny!" she said. "How are you?"

"Fine, Alice, very well, thank you," said Danny Dunham, waddling his bulk over to the counter, walking on amazingly small feet. Black aerated Oxford shoes, his usual dark blue suit, a red-and-black tie, a lush Windsor knot. He smiled, glancing around the shop, his eyes skipping over the rock-star posters to Fletch, who squatted by a carton near a revolving rack of T-shirts. "Good morning, Mr. Fletcher," he said.

"Hiya, Danny." Fletch sliced open the carton with a knife.

"What can I do for you, Danny?" Alice asked.

"Well . . ." His smile faltered, and immediately he looked uncomfortable.

"Is there something wrong?"

"No," he said. "Oh no, no. It's just that Mother . . ."

"I've been meaning to come by and see her," said Alice. "But I had so much catching up to do here."

Actually, she hadn't been meaning to go see Dead Mary at all. She just wanted to put the whole scary adventure behind her. And Mary Dunham was the last person she needed to see. For quite a while, at least.

"Of course, mother would love to see you anytime. She's quite fond of you, Alice, but . . . well, I'm really here about your brother."

"Ike?"

Danny nodded. He swallowed and looked away, just as Ike Fuelle stepped through the curtained-off doorway at the rear of the store. Danny blushed in embarrassment.

"Hey, Dan," Ike said. "I've been expecting you."

"You *have*?" said Alice.

Ike came around behind the counter, hit No Sale on the cash register, then peeled two tens and a five from the cash drawer.

Danny's humiliation deepened. "I'm afraid," he said, "that Mother said to tell you that she reconsidered and now feels *thirty*-five would be more appropriate. But," he added quickly, "if you don't have that much, twenty-five will be fine."

Ike pulled out another ten, and passed the four bills to Danny Dunham. "I'll pay you back," he said to Alice.

"Out of your first million," she said.

"Right," he said, laughing. "It comes right off the top."

After Danny Dunham had folded the money away in his billfold and gone, Ike grabbed his jean jacket from a peg on the wall and headed for the door. "Be back in an hour," he said.

"Where are you going?"

"Just out."

"Hey! If you don't have anything important to do, why don't you give me a hand sorting out these T-shirts," said Fletch.

"Who said I didn't have anything important to do?" Ike replied and left in a flash.

"Your brother's still a lazy bum," Fletch called to Alice.

She smiled, held Fletch's gaze for a long moment, then looked back down at her scratchpad. "Yeah," she said. "But I like him."

Bo Cudhy was standing outside the video store where he worked, talking on a cordless phone. "I checked the train schedule," he said. "And there's one that leaves Richmond at ten after seven. Gets you up here tomorrow just after lunch. Yeah?" His face brightened. "Yeah? Okay. Sure I'll meet you. You're really coming?" Bo laughed. "No," he said, "I'm not surprised or nothin'. I'm worth it." He laughed again, nodded, said, "See ya," pressed the disconnect button, and slammed down the antenna.

His smile stretched from ear to ear when he looked up and saw Ike Fuelle hurrying across Bowe Street.

"Hey! Ike!"

Ike glanced around, waved at Bo, but just kept on going.

His heart started pounding the first minute he was walking along the canal's towpath. As he came nearer to the spot where he'd arranged to meet Del for a picnic, his breath had become so shallow and rapid that he felt light-headed—like he was hyperventilating.

She did that to him.

It was amazing, but she did.

He stopped now, seeing her perched on the limestone mile-marker—just as she'd been that first day. Her back was turned to him, but he could see that she had her large, hollow-body guitar cradled against her.

She was playing something—no, *creating* something: she was picking out notes, stopping, picking out the same notes again. Then jotting them down on a piece of music-notation paper.

He wanted just to race up to her, so she would turn around and smile at him, tell him to sit down, listen to *this*. But he also wanted just to stand where he was, and watch her.

She was such a big mystery to him still.

The Orphan Del. From Milwaukee? Seattle? Detroit?

Or Bayonne, New Jersey?

A mystery. Such a mystery to him.

That spiky hair, that slender (currently emaciated) body, her brilliant smiles, her mournful stares.

Such a mystery.

And he loved it. Ike Fuelle loved it.

He called, "Hey Del!" then hurried over to her, realizing suddenly that he'd discovered, at last, what he really wanted to do for the rest of his life.

FICTION DE HAVEN
De Haven, Tom.
The orphan's tent /

OCEE LIBRARY

Atlanta-Fulton Public Library